Ayanami Rei Number Quatre
Rei Series Parallel Clone
Pilot of Eva Unit-0.0.

Ayanami Rei Number Cinq
Rei Series Parallel Clone
Pilot of Eva Unit-0.0.

Ayanami Rei Number Six
Rei Series Parallel Clone
Pilot of Eva Unit-0.0.

Aida Kensuke
Trainee, Nerv Japan Department
of Security Intelligence, Relic
Retrieval Unit.

SENGOKUHARA SENIOR HIGH SCHOOL
SECOND-YEAR STUDENTS

Now, at age 17—

Suzuhara Tōji
Somehow, he became a Nerv Japan Pilot Liaison Officer.

Ikari Shinji
Pilot of Eva Unit-01 Somehow, he became the class representative.

LOW PRIORITY

LOW PRIORITY

Soryu Asuka Langley
Pilot of Eva Unit-02.

Ayanami Rei Number Trois

The person consciously controlling Reis Quatre, Cinq, and Six. Pilot of Eva Unit-00 Type-F.

Horaki Hikari
Former class representative; current assistant class representative.

LOW PRIORITY

PRIORITY

LOW PRIORITY

LOW PRIORITY

LOW PRIORITY

LOW PRIORITY

EVANGELION ANIMA

Three years after the Battle at Nerv Headquarters...

The key to the Human Instrumentality Project, offered at the altar of light, was not Shinji, but rather Asuka and Eva Unit-02.

EVA UNIT-Ø1 TYPE-F

An experimental unit equipped with A.T. Field control technology. The Type-F unit is capable of A.T. Field-powered flight as was hoped, but the modifications enable a jumping ability beyond what the unit's form would suggest is possible, all while wearing stronger, heavier armor plating.

STD. EQUIPMENT

IMPACT BOLT: ELECTRICAL ANTIPHASE WEAPON

As the world rebuilds…

As the people settle back into peace…

The officers of Nerv remain in a state of unease.

From the rebuilt Hakone, from the bottom of the caldera that shelters them, they are frightened, unable to surrender their swords.

YPE: WIDE AREA CONTROL REVISION

UNIT-Ø.Ø

-0.0 units were launched into orbit
watch over the entire planet.

No one knows what the
future holds now that the
Human Instrumentality
Project has ended.

What should mankind do?

Is the threat really gone?

EVA-01 INTEGRATED BODY

This armor, with integrated restraints, was intended for Eva-01, but the plans were abandoned when the unit unexpectedly metamorphosed into Super Evangelion.

EVA-02 EQUIPPED WITH MICROWAVE
RECTENNA (SUPPLIED BY OUTSIDE GROUP)

Eva-02's heavily damaged head and body armor has been replaced with integrated restraint armor, but, along with Eva-00 Type-F, Eva-02 still relies on an outdated external power supply. Even so, the Eva has matured, along with its pilot, and the pair are the most skilled and trusted within Nerv Japan.

As with Type-1, these mass-production Evangelion corpses carry the cocoon of a larval Angel in their abdomens, but they have been equipped with an additional Q.R. Signum plate. The extra energy source gives them significantly greater power.

ANGEL CARRIER TYPE-2

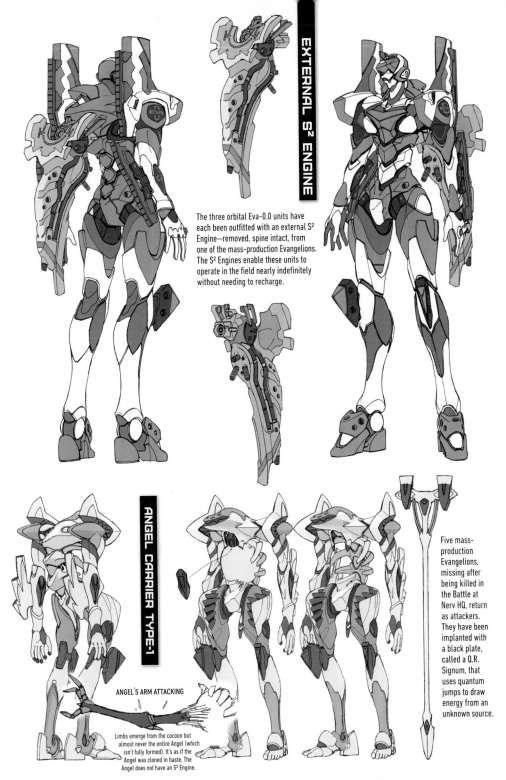

The three orbital Eva-0.0 units have each been outfitted with an external S² Engine—removed, spine intact, from one of the mass-production Evangelions. The S² Engines enable these units to operate in the field nearly indefinitely without needing to recharge.

ANGEL CARRIER TYPE-1

ANGEL'S ARM ATTACKING

Limbs emerge from the cocoon but almost never the entire Angel (which isn't fully formed). It's as if the Angel was cloned in haste. The Angel does not have an S² Engine.

Five mass-production Evangelions, missing after being killed in the Battle at Nerv HQ, return as attackers. They have been implanted with a black plate, called a Q.R. Signum, that uses quantum jumps to draw energy from an unknown source.

Super Evangelion

The birth of an Eva with a heart.

When Shinji awakens, Super Evangelion's visor opens.

NEON GENESIS EVANGELION ANIMA

VOLUME 1

BY
Ikuto Yamashita

CONCEPT
Khara

PLANNING & EDITING
Yasuo Kashihara

Seven Seas Entertainment

EVANGELION ANIMA VOL. 1

©khara

First published in Japan in 2017 by
KADOKAWA CORPORATION, Tokyo.
English translation rights arranged with
KADOKAWA CORPORATION, Tokyo.

Seven Seas press and purchase enquiries can be sent to
Marketing Manager Lianne Sentar at press@gomanga.com.
Information requiring the distribution and purchase of
digital editions is available from Digital Manager CK Russell
at digital@gomanga.com.

Follow Seven Seas Entertainment online at
sevenseasentertainment.com.

TRANSLATION: Nathan Collins
ADAPTATION: Peter Adrian Behravesh
COVER DESIGN: KC Fabellon
INTERIOR LAYOUT & DESIGN: Clay Gardner
PROOFREADER: Jade Gardner, Dayna Abel
LIGHT NOVEL EDITOR: Nibedita Sen
MANAGING EDITOR: Julie Davis
EDITOR-IN-CHIEF: Adam Arnold
PUBLISHER: Jason DeAngelis

ISBN: 978-1-64275-708-8
Printed in Canada
First Printing: October 2019
10 9 8 7 6 5 4 3 2 1

ANIMA

CONTENTS

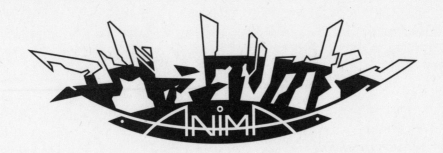

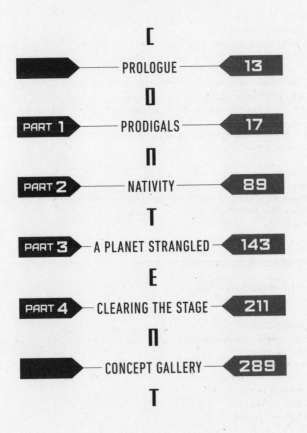

NEON GENESIS
EVANGELION ANIMA

NOTHING WENT as planned.

It was to be the end of mankind as a collective of individual beings. The Geofront opened its mouth to the sky, but the band of mass-production Evangelions encircled Eva-02—not Shinji's Eva-01.

At the commencement of the Human Instrumentality Project's final ritual, with Asuka and her Evangelion at its center, Eva-01 emerged from a hard-won fight against the enemy forces assaulting Nerv HQ and disrupted this ritual.

The tree of life, which had materialized in the sky when the Lance of Longinus pierced Eva-02, now crumbled, the Human Instrumentality Project terminated by Shinji's hand.

This is where *ANIMA* begins.

Eva-01 cupped its hands together, as if scooping up water, and raised them to the clear, blue sky. From Katsuragi Misato's perspective on the ground, the giant's gesture seemed like a supplication.

"What are you holding?" she asked and then prompted, "Shinji-kun?"

Realizing he'd been asked a question, Eva-01's pilot replied through the external speaker.

《I found Kaji-san's field—his watermelons.》

During the Battle at Nerv HQ, the Geofront's dome ceiling had collapsed onto the subsurface, the tranquil, subterranean space devastated by bombs—courtesy of the Japan Strategic Self-Defense Force—and gusts of wind from the swarm of mass-production Evangelions.

The watermelon patch's survival was nothing short of a miracle.

The dome's collapse had blanketed the subsurface with a layer of ash-colored dust and debris, crumbled bits of the armored ceiling and the buildings of the city above. Only chance had left this particular patch of land identifiable—a broken garden faucet spraying a tall fountain of water.

Shinji gently brushed away the dust and found the watermelon leaves and vines still alive.

Before the battle, the child pilot had been taking care of the field in its owner's absence.

《I don't suppose I should replant the field where it was, should I?》

"Honestly, no." Misato gestured to the concrete dome, currently under construction, that would soon cover the old Nerv HQ and its surroundings. "Once the dome is finished, there'll be no sky. And without reflecting arrays, sunlight won't reach down here. After the new above-ground HQ is built, the Geofront will be closed off."

《Yeah, I figured. That's why I'm going to move the field to the surface.》

"What did Ryoji say about that idea?"

《He said I could do whatever I wanted.》

He'd also added, "After all, your choice created this world." But Shinji left that part out.

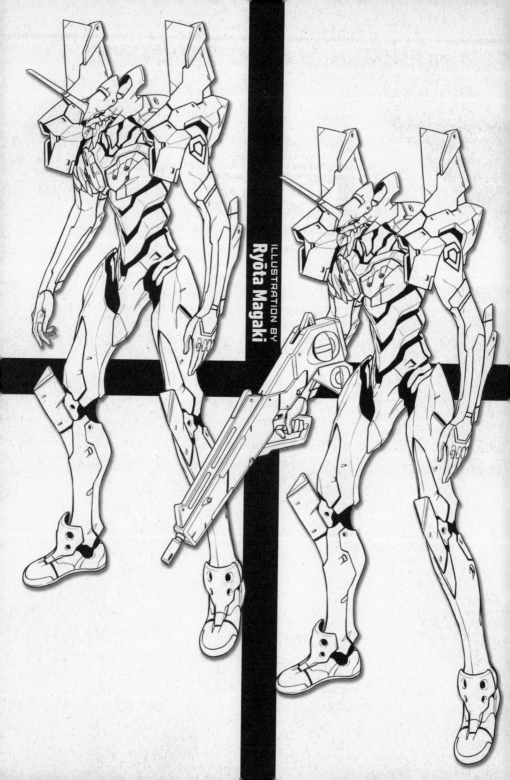

ILLUSTRATION BY
Ryōta Magaki

PART 1

NEON GENESIS
PRODIGALS
EVANGELION: ANIMA

NEON GENESIS
EVANGELION ANIMA

CHAPTER 1

— SENTINELS OF THE BIOSPHERE

THREE UNIT-0.0 EVANGELIONS orbited the Earth. From this high up, the full horizon formed a closed blue disc that fit neatly into their field of view.

The former Unit-00 Evas had been redesigned for operation in space, including external S^2 Engines to free them from outside power sources. Evenly spaced 120 degrees apart along the same orbit, the three units formed the points of a triangle that enveloped the Earth.

A clone of Ayanami Rei rode inside each Eva-0.0. They'd been cultivated in artificial wombs and assigned numbers: Quatre, Cinq, and Six. Now they slept, eyes half-closed, in their individual entry plugs. They slumbered in tranquility, almost as if time had stopped around them.

A fluid called LCL flowed gently through the entry plugs to deliver oxygen to the pilots' lungs. The girls looked like delicate dolls as they slept in their aquariums, their hair undulating in the LCL. The chests of their white plugsuits held a resin-based muscular mechanism that slowly tightened and relaxed in rhythm with their breathing to help their lungs cycle the thick liquid.

The circulation pumps whirred faintly.

The external S^2 Engines let out a distant hum as they idled.

Together with the girls, the Evas formed a monitoring and interception system.

And the clones' quiet slumber signified that the world was currently at peace.

Most of the corpses of the nine Seele mass-production Evas that assaulted Nerv HQ went missing after their defeat, vanishing either in transit or at their destination. After the nullification of the Human Instrumentality Project, the missing mass-production Evas became the greatest threat to global security.

Three mass-production units were recovered from the battlefield—Nerv HQ—and promptly disassembled. Nerv engineers salvaged their S^2 Engines and later installed them on the backs of the Series-00 Eva units modified for zero-G and zero-atmosphere operation.

These new Eva units, designated Series-0.0, were sent into orbit and tasked with finding and eradicating the remaining mass-production Evas.

Perhaps there was some irony in using Evas that operated on power sources reclaimed from their companions' carcasses for this mission, but regardless, the S^2 Engines freed the Series-0.0

units from umbilical power and enabled them to operate without support for extended periods.

When instructed, the Rei clones could awaken in roughly ten seconds. In thirty seconds, the Eva-0.0 units could rev up from an idle state to combat readiness. And in ninety, they could take aim with their long-barreled gamma-ray laser cannons and fire at any target that was within their field of view— and some that weren't, as the lasers could penetrate up to a depth of 500 meters.

By maintaining their equidistant orbits, the three Eva-0.0 units monitored the entire surface of the Earth, their eyes and ears vigilant to all forms of communication.

They were a global anti-Angel search-and-destroy network constructed with the full efforts of Nerv—now restructured as Nerv Japan—and its leader, Katsuragi Misato.

Up to now, the global community had abided the existence of the Evangelions because, despite their overwhelming power, they were ultimately ground-based weapons operated from a small island nation whose borders restricted their range. Once in low Earth orbit, however, these same weapons represented total air supremacy. But despite protests of sovereign infringement, Commander Katsuragi pushed forward unilaterally with her orbital defense strategy, backed by the true might—and implied threat—of the Evas.

Misato took great pains to emphasize, formally and in writing, that the mission's only goal was to prevent the revival of the mass-production Evas. But such efforts were futile; the nations of the world couldn't help but see a threat.

The Human Instrumentality Project had been thwarted. But what would come next? No one could say.

Former Nerv Commander Ikari Gendo and Dr. Akagi Ritsuko had disappeared during the battle, along with the project's key conspirators. Vice Commander Fuyutsuki Kozo had resigned with hardly a word. But even if they'd still been around, they wouldn't have had a better grasp of the future than anyone else. This was uncharted territory.

Though the world was easing into a time of peace, vigilance sometimes necessitated force, even absent the Angels' threat. Under Misato's command, the personnel of Nerv Japan, and everyone involved with the use and development of Evangelions, were keenly aware that the outside world hated them more with each passing day. Despite this, they clung to the hope that all their worry and preparation would be for nothing.

Three years had passed since the Battle at Nerv HQ, and it was three years that Nerv, and the world, had needed.

The three Eva-0.0 units floated above the Earth with their heads pointing down and their parasols facing the sun. As they flew, they scanned the outer reaches of the atmosphere with powerful sensors in their heads and receptor arrays in their shoulders. They transmitted the data they collected back to Nerv Japan HQ, all while carrying the half-asleep Reis inside.

Ayanami Rei's physical body could be duplicated from her DNA, but there could only be one Ayanami Rei conscious at a time.

This seemed to be the rule; the third and current Rei hadn't awakened until the second had perished in the battle with the Angel Armisael.

But the soulless, *in vitro* Reis exhibited a curious synchronicity in motion and brain activity with the third Rei—the one possessing a soul. Further examination had led to a method of mental mirroring that allowed Rei to control her clones.

The current Rei was given a number—Number Trois—and became the primary Rei, with the three soulless clones—Number Quatre, Number Cinq, and Number Six—as her secondaries, whom she could control as extensions of her limbs, senses, and thoughts.

This ability came as a result of training rather than technology, and at present, no known method existed to sever their connection. Furthermore, communication between the Reis occurred instantaneously, giving them the distinct advantage of being able to respond rapidly to any emergency.

There was a catch—maintaining the consciousness of four beings with one soul wore on the primary Rei. And so the three clones remained in light slumber.

By imagining herself transferring her consciousness, Rei Trois could awaken the orbiting clones from the ground at will.

Not long ago, Rei Trois had landed the Series-0.0 Evas one at a time at the Tanegashima Space Center, where they were refitted with upgraded restraint armor before launching them back into orbit.

Even during that process, the sentinels remained half-asleep unless Rei Trois willed them to wake.

The three clones also shared senses and could form memories from the experiences of the others.

The arrangement was a system of "one plus three" but with only one soul.

No more children would be made into Eva pilots. This was not only Nerv Japan's decision but also Rei's personal hope. As of this year, all the fourteen-year-old children who'd been chosen to pilot Evas, including Rei, were now seventeen.

CHAPTER 2

SUPER EVANGELION

"**G**UYS," ASUKA SAID, "how about you go change your clothes?"

Shinji and Toji had just arrived on the top deck of the command center and were still in their school uniforms. The two young men met the suggestion with confused looks.

"No," Shinji replied, "I think I'd rather finish this conversation first."

They were talking about Eva-01 getting refitted with the new restraint armor, like Eva-02 and the Series-0.0 Evas.

"There's no way we're calling it 'super.'" Toji said. "Hey, what are you laughing at?"

Asuka snickered. She'd already changed out of her school clothes and into a tank top, and her bare shoulders shook. "Super... Super Evangelion? Dun-dada-dunnn!"

Asuka's rendition of a superhero's fanfare echoed throughout the quiet command center, and several technicians on the middle and lower decks looked up. Some even chuckled.

"Well, *I* think it's great, Misato," Asuka said. "It sounds utterly idiotic—perfect for Unit One! Let's go with that name, but just for Unit One."

Sitting in her chair on the top deck, Misato looked genuinely confused—she hadn't been joking about the name. Shinji and Toji were not amused.

"Is the name that weird?" Misato asked. "I thought it was pretty common to take the old name and put 'super' in front when a weapon gets an upgrade."

"It's not weird," Asuka replied cheerfully. "It's perfect!"

Toji jabbed a finger at her. "Shut up. Try developing your brain for a change instead of your chest."

"Hmph! Well, where's *your* brain, huh? Did you leave it in your old arms and legs?"

She thrust her body forward so that Toji's extended finger was a hair's breadth away from touching the swell of her tank top.

Toji panicked and pulled his hand back. Asuka snorted.

"That's not fair!" he complained.

"You stink of sweat. Go take a shower. Better make it a cold one." The red-haired girl gave a mean-spirited laugh.

The boys were exercising in the facility's gym.

They were both self-conscious of their actions.

Shinji had chosen a new destiny for the world in ways both monumental and small, from thwarting the Human Instrumentality Project to relocating Kaji's watermelon patch.

Before beginning his workout, Toji had fine-tuned the sizing of his cybernetic limbs and double-checked their synchronization.

Toji's body had suffered severe injuries in the fight against the Angel Bardiel. The doctors had replaced his heart with one grown in a lab, but they'd given up on regenerating his arms and legs. The first time they'd attempted to attach a regrown set of limbs, Bardiel, from out of nowhere, had re-manifested somehow, and the Angel's contagion had shown signs of returning. Apparently, the intact form of the human body, or that of an Evangelion, could trigger the Angel's activation. In the end, the greatest minds at Nerv had been unable to eliminate the risk of Bardiel reactivating within Toji's body, and so the boy was given mechanical limbs.

Toji was struck from the pilot roster, but since he was going to be under strict Nerv surveillance for the foreseeable future no matter what, he decided to take an active role in the organization. He was granted high-level security clearance and began working as a liaison between the pilots. If nothing else, he needed the money; maintaining robotic limbs wasn't cheap.

"Hey, Shinji," Toji said, "have you seen the SSDF's giant robot?"

"You mean the one in Gotemba? It's about half as tall as Jet Alone and built like a tank."

"I hear it's even stronger than Jet Alone. And it can fly, too."

The robot was designed to combat individual, large-scale threats. It had been named Akashima after an old word for typhoon.

Unlike Evangelions, which grew into humanoid shapes for reasons not understood by science, the N_2 Reactor-powered Akashima was humanoid by design. Its legs could traverse any terrain, and its arms allowed it to hold weapons, to fire in any direction, and—at least theoretically—to pin down an unruly opponent in close combat. Its body offered more than mere structural support; it provided a frame for protective armor and could withstand unexpected impacts if necessary. Depending on its configuration, the Akashima could even fly, which improved the Japan Strategic Self-Defense Force's ability to respond to developing situations quickly.

But, most incredibly, the robot could do all of this without external support.

"It must be nice to be able to fly," Shinji said.

"The thing can't fly high," Toji responded, a bit defensively. "It relies on the ground effect."

"Sure, but I bet it can cruise really fast."

"Don't sound so excited. Publicly, sure, it's an anti-Angel mech designed to support the Evas, but..." Toji lowered his voice, despite no one being around to overhear. "A lot of folks are wondering if maybe it's designed to *get rid* of the Evas."

Shinji didn't follow. "I know the Evas aren't exactly popular, given how expensive they are to run, but—" He suddenly understood. "Oh! Is that why you think the robot's been stationed so close to us?"

"After all the trouble the SSDF caused in the Battle at Nerv HQ, Misato-san went to a lot of effort to get the Japanese government to acknowledge the Hakone caldera as UN-leased territory. Remember, we're an extraterritorial zone. Maybe the governments on the outside don't like it. Maybe they're looking for a way to take it back."

"Maybe... Does that mean they're watching us from the caldera's rim?"

By possessing six Eva units—Unit-01 Type-F, Unit-00 Type-F, Unit-02, and the three Series-0.0 units stationed in orbit—Nerv Japan had arguably become the most powerful military force on the planet. Four of the Evas—Unit-00 Type-F and Unit-02 excluded—had S^2 Engines. Unit-01 had ingested one when the Eva went berserk against the Angel Zeruel, and the Series-0.0 units had been outfitted with engines harvested from the mass-production Evas after the Battle at Nerv HQ. These four Evas could now operate in combat nearly indefinitely.

"That's why Unit One is getting upgraded to Super Evangelion," Toji said.

"There'll be no 'super' anything, Toji. I'm sure this restraint armor upgrade idea will get dropped. It's not suited for Unit One."

"Right. It's more for Unit Two and Unit Zero, seeing as how Soryu and Ayanami have developed their Evas' bodies over time, with their waists narrowing and their... Uh..."

Toji gestured to indicate how the shape of the Evas' bodies had changed, but he fell into an awkward silence as he realized his motion also mirrored how Asuka's and Ayanami's bodies had developed.

Evas could alter their own physical configuration. Though constructed out of inorganic matter, every now and then, the giants behaved as if they were living beings. Sometimes these changes came swiftly and drasticly, like when they suffered heavy damage while in synchronization with their pilot, but other times the transformation came gradually while in their cages at night accompanied by a grinding noise. This phenomenon caused no end of grief to the maintenance teams, but Ibuki Maya, current chief of the science and engineering divisions, speculated that the process was part of the Evas' natural development.

In the three years since the Battle at Nerv HQ, this gradual growth became more noticeable. The mysterious presence inside each Eva came to the surface only rarely now, and the pilots themselves had begun to influence the physical characteristics of their Evas. This had most strongly manifested in Asuka and Eva-02.

Asuka's body had developed—not just in the volume of her bust, but in her shoulders, arms, waist, legs—into a graceful and slender physique. When she walked by, red hair bouncing, hips swaying, utterly self-assured, anyone might turn their head and wonder, *Is she a model?*

But it was more than the passing of time that had matured her. Her confidence had grown. She used to claim that she was the best pilot, her boasts a manifestation of her insecurity. These days, though she still spoke harshly to others, she was harshest on herself.

I won't be careless—not with my missions or in my day-to-day life.

Her acerbity had been a source of stress, but it had also led to a sense of fulfillment.

Her growth, both physical and mental, had changed the shape and structure of her Eva. At a certain point, Eva-02's restraint armor no longer fit despite the best efforts of the mechanics. The armor was removed, and new, properly fitting, Stage 2 restraint armor was created.

After the replacement armor showed improved performance, it was installed on Ayanami's Eva-00—though not the Unit-00 Type-F—and the three orbiting Series-0.0 units, which had been landed, one by one, at Tanegashima Space Center for the refitting before returning to orbit.

Ayanami had grown, too, if not to the same extent as Asuka. Still, a pilot's self-identity determined their Eva's form. Eva-00 could have fit into just about any new armor, since even after three years, Rei's sense of identity remained stunted.

"By the way," Toji said to Shinji, "why are you avoiding Ayanami?"

The sudden change of topic caught Shinji off guard. Toji was referring to the Ayanami who had been with them since the Battle at Nerv HQ—Trois.

In the wake of the battle, the fact that Ayanami had been cloned from Shinji's mother became public knowledge. For many, this served as confirmation of a vague, but firmly held, suspicion. As such, the truth was quickly accepted.

Shinji struggled with the revelation for several days but ultimately told Rei that she was her own person. That should have settled the matter, and yet...

"I'm not avoiding her," Shinji said. "If I see her, I say hello, and... Oh, right! We talk about work, too."

"Yeah?" From what Toji had observed, Shinji was lying.

"Yeah."

"If you say so," Toji said. "All this talk of new armor reminds me—that huge one is still in the underground strata where Ritsuko-san left it, right?"

"It's high-spec, but I'd bet that armor's even heavier than it looks. At least as heavy as the Type-F. Plus, it's lacking in so many—" Shinji cut himself off and peered at Toji quizzically. "Hang on. Your clearance doesn't allow you down there!"

Irritated, Toji looked away. "If you don't want it, then it's gonna be Stage 2 for you."

"I don't see the problem," Asuka said, appearing behind Shinji. She must have heard Toji talking about the Stage 2 armor. "You're skinny enough. You fit into my plugsuit before, didn't you?"

She lifted Shinji's shirt up—only to be annoyed by what she found. *Since when did that little brat's back get so wide?* He even had muscles now.

"How long ago was that?" Shinji asked. "And why are you mad at me?"

"Shut up!" Asuka crossed her arms.

"Where's Ayanami?" Toji asked.

"She said there was a student council meeting after school today."

CHAPTER 3

THE FALLEN

T HE TRANQUILITY above the skies broke without warning. Rei Quatre's eyelids twitched open, drawing back the long eyelashes that had shrouded her view. On the surface below, Rei Trois saw the expansive blue planet through Quatre's eyes.

Softly, Trois said, "What?"

Eva-0.0's visual sensors could resolve detail at a resolution of less than ten centimeters and could perform real-time filtering of moving objects larger than five meters. Quatre's Eva focused on a harbor, then filtered out the movement of its structures and equipment and that of the large ocean mammals in its waters. An unidentifiable object remained. The object didn't appear to be a threat, but Quatre felt—if only vaguely—disquieted.

The primary Rei sent her thoughts out to her clones.

"We have no physical data. Should we conclude that this is an error?"

《Cinq reserves judgment.》

《Six acknowledges the error.》

《*Trois reserves judgment.*》

《Quatre will perform a more detailed examination, including environmental data.》

Rei Trois was walking home from school. She wore the white summer uniform of Tokyo-3's private high school. Her feet, at the ends of her long, light-skinned legs, beat a quiet, steady rhythm on the pavement...until they didn't. The pale fairy of a girl stood suddenly still, and her briefcase clattered to the ground.

The sun had set over the light rail station, but its heat lingered. Rei Trois gripped herself by the shoulders and watched as the doors of the train bound for Nerv HQ closed in front of her. The train glided away, leaving her behind.

She had a tendency to keep her eyes half-lidded, but now they were open wide.

"What...?"

She felt beads of sweat trickling down her skin.

Her breathing became ragged—unusual for her—and her chest rose and fell heavily. When she spoke, it came out as an uncharacteristic scream.

"Help!"

Something pitch-black flowed into her.

She felt a strange force pulling at her limbs, and then it was gone, leaving her with the shock of its absence.

"I can't hear my other selves."

Suddenly, she was alone.

She found herself crouching on the train platform while students wearing the same uniform as her came running, summoned by her scream.

An alarm sounded throughout the command center.

Nerv Japan HQ was in turmoil. The three Series-0.0 Evas had been orbiting the globe for two years without incident, but now one—piloted by Rei Quatre—had deviated from its prescribed orbit and started losing altitude.

Some officers shouted reports as others streamed in from the cafeteria. "We're no longer receiving telemetry! Quatre's status is unknown!"

"Commander on deck!"

Heads turned as Katsuragi Misato barked, "Stop your work!"

As order returned to the room, the commander strode across the top deck and called out loud enough for Hyuga Makoto on the middle deck to hear. "What's the status of Rei Quatre?"

Hyuga was a bookish but highly capable technician who'd been a fixture in the command center back when Nerv Japan was just Nerv. "She's not responding to comms!" he said. "Vitals unknown."

"Is Rei Trois still at school?" Misato asked. "See if she can make contact with Quatre."

From the same middle deck, the dutiful-if-distant Aoba Shigeru replied with information he'd just received. "The security intelligence division has recovered Rei Trois on her way home from school. They say she's not in her right mind."

"What?"

Trois had been their last hope of finding out what was happening with Quatre.

"Rei Cinq and Rei Six are in a state of confusion," Aoba said. "Their vitals are unstable. I recommend we administer sedation."

"Make it happen," Misato said. "Can their observational equipment get a visual on Quatre's Eva?"

Cinq's and Six's Evas should have been able to see Quatre at the boundary of the upper atmosphere. A technician applied a digital mask to darken the Earth, and a faintly glimmering light became visible at its edge.

"Those look like scattering fragments," Aoba said. "AI spectral analysis confirms they belong to Quatre's Eva."

Shinji's voice came over the comms. 《This is Shinji in the cage. I'm hearing that one of the Ayanamis got shot down!》

From the fragments, that certainly seemed to be the case.

"It's too soon to say," Misato replied. "There might have been an accident. We still don't know."

"What about the rooftop cameras?" Misato asked. "Pull up the tower's all-sky observation camera, A1."

A technician routed the incoming feed from the observation team to the main screen.

"That's Unit-0.0's FSB flare!" Misato said.

The cross-shaped flare, violent, bright, and pulsing, was visible in the twilight. The FSB—or Field Stepping Booster—utilized an A.T. Field for direction and blasts from the N_2 Reactor for power—enough to lift the Evas into orbit.

Was Quatre trying to accelerate back into position?

"No, the opposite!" Misato realized. "The Eva is rocketing itself east. It's decelerating!"

Unit Quatre was firing in the reverse direction of its orbit.

The cross-shaped light slowed to a stop above Hakone and then winked out.

"Unit-0.0 has disengaged its FSB!" Hyuga said. "The Eva has lost its orbital velocity and is now directly overhead. Relative velocity zero."

"And that means…?"

"The Eva is following a steep downward trajectory that matches the Earth's rotation. It's falling straight onto our heads!"

"Could the Eva burn up?" Misato asked.

Aoba replied, "Even if its A.T. Field is inoperable—and we don't know that to be the case—the Eva won't burn in the upper atmosphere. Besides, its orbital deceleration is already complete. If, however, the Unit-0.0 breaches the denser air of the stratosphere, the resulting shock wave could damage a wide area and penetrate deep underground."

Is this a malfunction, or is Rei Quatre doing this intentionally? Either way, I need to take action now.

Misato reached a decision.

"I'm declaring this an accidental loss of orbit. Issue an emergency order to all sectors of Tokyo-3 and the surrounding municipalities! All residents must be evacuated to the underground shelters. Prepare for impact! Has there been any response from Rei Quatre?"

"We're still trying to contact her," one of the other technicians said, "but there's no response."

If the Eva is going to fall here, then...

"Shinji-kun, Asuka," Misato ordered, "begin your entry sequence. Start up Unit One and Unit Two!"

The giants' supports released. Shinji and Asuka had been waiting for the command; they immediately readied their Evas.

"Unit One," Misato continued, "use your A.T. Field to absorb the Eva-0.0's momentum at the projected point of impact! Just like you did with the Angel."

Compared to the Angel Sahaquiel, which Shinji had successfully caught, the Series-0.0 Eva had less mass. More importantly, Eva-01 had gained an S^2 Engine since that encounter and could now produce a far more powerful A.T. Field. Over the past three years, Shinji had trained hard to learn how to use it.

So why did he feel so uneasy? Was it because of how long it had been since he'd responded to an emergency?

《This is Shinji in Unit One. Understood!》

"Asuka, we're going to change your position a little. Deploy to the sniping post at Mount Komagatake."

Mount Komagatake was one of many peaks near the center of the Hakone caldera. In a previous battle, Mount Kami, the tallest of these peaks, had been destroyed. Now Mount Komagatake was the tallest. The sniping post there provided a strategic anti-air position, commanding a clear view over the caldera that served as Tokyo-3's home.

The mountain was located roughly 4.5 kilometers from Nerv HQ. Between the two, on the eastern side of Lake Ashi, rugged, mountainous terrain impeded above-ground travel, but high-speed Eva transport tunnels underground made the trip a straight shot. Even Evangelions that still relied on umbilical power could rapidly deploy to the sniping post.

《This is Asuka in Unit Two. Understood!》

Alarms sounded throughout the city for the first time in three years. Inside Nerv HQ's command center, Aoba held the external comms line to his ear as he looked over his shoulder.

"The SSDF out of Matsushiro is offering their support. They've sent a live feed of Unit Quatre from the Tokachi air defense site."

"Is it just me," Misato said, "or does it sound like they're saying, 'serves you right'?"

"If only. They probably think we're staging the whole thing."

Misato could imagine the accusations: after three years without any Angels or mass-production Evas, Nerv Japan had staged an incident to justify their continued existence.

"Tell their officers they are welcome to come observe, if they have the guts to enter the impact zone. And warn them that their forces are not to cross the border into the caldera."

When the Series-0.0 Eva crossed into the E layer of the ionosphere—the altitude where shooting stars glowed incandescent—a plume of white smoke enveloped the giant. Had some part of the Eva succumbed to the air resistance and scattered like so many flower petals? Was it the gamma-ray laser cannon's hardpoint, or visual sensor panels from the parasol, or something else?

The buildings of Tokyo-3 began to sink into the ground, to protect against the impact's shock wave.

Shinji said, "If we can catch the falling Eva, the buildings will hold, but if we fail, the damage could extend underground."

《Command center to Unit One: Be advised, the predicted impact point has moved to the former location of Owakudani!》

"Unit One. Acknowledged!"

The ground rumbled as Eva-01 sprinted east from where it had surfaced near the center of Nerv HQ. The heavily armored Type-F unit had been outfitted with jump jets in its knee shields, which it used to hurtle over the city's many above-ground light rail lines.

The present-day HQ facility resembled a half-buried sphere, neatly filling the hole that the mass-production Evas had blasted in the roof of the Geofront. In its center was a tall shaft, though the opening didn't provide a view of the old Nerv headquarters. Instead, it offered three hundred meters of empty space that led to a gigantic white dome—nicknamed "the Sarcophagus"—which covered the underground world. Beneath the outer layer of the dome's HTC—Hard Tektite Concrete, a strongly bonding, glass-like concrete—were several layers of armor plating followed by even more HTC on the bottom. All these layers worked together to form a secure seal over the former Nerv HQ.

《Command center to Unit One. Shinji-kun, can your Eva get a visual on the falling Unit-0.0?》

Eva-01 applied its brakes and looked upward. A tiny blotch appeared high in the evening sky, the fading sunlight illuminating the falling Series-0.0 Eva on one side. The image transmitting from Eva-01's eyes was magnified and shaky. Shinji willed himself to stay perfectly still.

"Just barely! I'll try to concentrate."

A.T. Fields were the walls that enclosed every person and, as such, could generally only be put up around one's self. Generating an A.T. Field at a remote location was possible, but there were limits—and the difficulty increased with distance.

"Focusing A.T. Field."

Given careful concentration, the characteristics of the wall of the self had a certain amount of flexibility. Eva-01 raised its hands to the sky. Shinji usually found the most success by picturing himself in the remote location, particularly if there was an object present that he could focus on. He would *feel* as if he were physically there to catch Quatre.

Though the falling Eva was still a great distance away, Shinji had a direct line of sight. The human mind was highly visual, and even a single thin wall between him and the Eva would have made concentrating far more difficult.

"Focusing in three, two, one—mark!"

The command center's main screen showed a live feed from the Nerv HQ telescope, which captured the faint, wispy A.T. Field manifesting in midair and the falling Eva-0.0 colliding with it—and effortlessly piercing through.

"Unit One, first remote ATF generated," Hyuga reported.

"That didn't even absorb two percent of the Eva's velocity," Misato said. "We've got a long way to go!"

"Unit Quatre is entering the D layer!"

"Shinji," Misato said, "at this rate, you'll to have to focus at least three more times. Slow that Eva down as much as you can before it enters the troposphere."

She didn't add, *If you don't, the shock wave will wreak widespread destruction.*

《This is Unit Two. I've arrived at the Mount Komagatake sniping post. Commencing with remote A.T. Field creation.》

"We'll do it together," Shinji replied. "I'll go on your signal."

《You'll *what?* As if you're good enough to match my timing! No, *you* do the countdown!》

Unlike Eva-01, Eva-02 still had to drag along an umbilical cable. Its power, movement, and operational time couldn't match an Eva with an S^2 Engine on board. But Asuka's unit excelled at tasks that required precision.

Eva-02 had lost two of its four eyes to a head wound in the Battle at Nerv HQ, and the giant now wore a two-eyed mask, like

Eva-01. But those two eyes zoomed in on the falling Eva-0.0 with perfect clarity.

"I wish I still had four eyes," Asuka said.

Eva-02 raised its hands to the heavens.

"Ready to try again, Super Shinji?"

《Could you not?》

A ripple appeared around Quatre's Eva.

This isn't good.

From the command center, Hyuga reported, 《Unit Quatre is entering the stratosphere!》

White smoke billowed from the Series-0.0 Eva. Shinji let out a deep breath and locked Eva-01's eyes on his target.

"Focus," he told himself. "Focus."

Meanwhile, Asuka was concentrating on the same point in the sky.

"I'm not sending myself there," she said under her breath. "I *am* there, standing in its path!"

She took slow, steady breaths as she waited for the signal.

"Mark!"

The A.T. Field was still faint, but now the shield had two layers generated by two Evas.

On the main screen in the command center, Unit Quatre suddenly appeared to have been struck by a large force and was thrown off course.

With satisfaction, Hyuga reported, "Command to Units One

and Two. Nice work. You've absorbed a significant amount of the Eva's kinetic energy! If you can do that one more time—"

In a sweeping motion, the Series-0.0 Eva reoriented itself.

"What the hell?!" Hyuga exclaimed.

Hearing his outburst, Aoba, who was coordinating the city's evacuation and shelter, looked up at the main screen and said, "The Eva isn't just in free fall? It's a controlled descent?!"

"The Eva's trajectory has changed!" Hyuga shouted, "The predicted impact is now five kilometers south—the middle of Lake Ashi!"

Not missing a beat, Misato said, "Asuka, you're closer!"

《Leave it to me!》

"Unit One—start running!"

Eva-01 Type-F sprinted into the dense forest at the base of Mount Daigatake, which stood between it and the new predicted point of impact.

A.T. Fields had another quirk: No matter how weakened an Eva or its pilot might have been, there was one place they could generate a field without fail—the ground beneath their feet. Otherwise, the hundred-meter-tall giants wouldn't have been able to walk across any stretch of ground—no matter how well engineered or fortified—without sinking.

That might sound too convenient to be plausible, but former Nerv executives had taken the phenomenon very seriously, and they'd left their records behind for the current staff.

The limits of the human form—

Humans cannot escape the ground. We are destined to crawl around in the dirt forever—to smear ourselves with it.

According to them, this quirk of the A.T. Fields was proof of our fate.

At the time, Asuka had said, "Duh, isn't that obvious?"

Eva-01 cut a path through the trees at full speed.

I have to make it!

Shinji neared Lake Ashi's eastern edge. The mountain used to run down into the water here, but after so many battles with the Angels, the forest had been completely burned down, leaving the mountain bare, and the land had collapsed on a large scale. The rugged rises and falls had shallowed out, and the few remaining trees were stunted and withered things. Eva-01 bounded over them and reached the lake's shore.

The Eva made one last, large jump toward a floating dock that extended out into the lake. The Type-F's sharp, backswept edges dragged little streaks of clouds with them, producing dissonant low- and high-pitched sounds as the Eva sliced through the air.

Resembling an animated suit of armor, the Type-F had been designed to test A.T. Field generation technology. Nerv Japan hoped that artificial deflection of A.T. Fields would lead not only to increased defensive capabilities but the ability to fly. Ultimately, flight hadn't been possible, but the Type-F's heavy restraint armor was more than upgraded plating; it allowed the unit's field-assisted jumps to cover a tremendous range. Watching the heavily armored Eva far outstrip the jumping capabilities of the lighter, sleeker models was a surreal experience.

The floating dock was a series of wafers with hollows in between, and when Eva-01 landed, it became a massive drum echoing through the mountains. The Eva activated its brakes to halt its momentum, and a shrill, metallic cry reverberated across the water's surface. Heavy anchor cables held the dock in place, but as the Eva landed, several snapped, kicking up large columns of water.

Quatre's Eva faced the heavens as it fell, the giant reflecting the sunset's afterglow.

《Now!》 Asuka's voice rattled through the hydrospeaker, and a new field generated by Eva-02 opened in the sky just in time for the Series-0.0 Eva to break through it.

"I'll catch you, Ayanami!"

Rei Quatre broke her silence with a single sentence.

《That's a lie.》

Before Shinji could generate another remote A.T. Field, Quatre created one of her own—strong, like a wall.

"What?" Shinji shouted.

Rei Quatre's voice was weak and raspy, but Shinji heard her clearly. When she spoke, he felt as if all other sounds had vanished.

Asuka sensed something unpleasant was about to happen.

Eva-02 reacted immediately, without waiting for Asuka's input, and leaped backward.

In the next instant, Asuka felt searing pain on the tip of her nose, and the spot where her Eva had been standing became blindingly bright.

"Eva-0.0 has fired!" Asuka shouted. Then she added accusingly, "Why?!"

There was a tremendous crash and Asuka was knocked backward.

The sniping post at Mount Komagatake had been constructed for Rei Trois' Eva-00 Type-F, which had been equipped with a special artillery rifle, the A.T. Field Piercer, at the cost of a literal arm and a leg. As such, the post had been built to withstand all manner of explosions as well as the Angels' highly penetrative attacks.

Now its layers of armor plating melted like butter.

Asuka screamed.

A ray of purple light fell across the peak of the tallest mountain south of Tokyo-3, followed by a large explosion.

The Nerv HQ building that housed the command center was protected under layers of heavy armor, and the structure had been designed to absorb earthquakes and other shocks, but the rumble still came up from below.

"The sniping post is under attack!" Hyuga declared

The room erupted as technicians began speaking over each other.

"Was that the Eva-0.0's gamma-ray laser cannon?"

"How far underground did the blast go?"

"What about Unit Two?" Misato asked. "What about Asuka? Is her Eva damaged?!"

The commander looked at the main screen, but the picture had gone blank.

"The explosion created an electromagnetic pulse," Hyuga said. "All systems are down! Reboot external communications, the monitors...everything!"

This temporary disconnection from the outside world might as well have been endless. Battles like this were measured in nano-seconds; everything would be over in half a minute. And for the rest of that time, the command center would be cut off.

The eradicated mountaintop stood to the east of Eva-01.

"Quatre? Asuka?!" Shinji cried out.

Several orange alert windows appeared on the plug's display to announce that his battle comms, data link, and several sensors had been temporarily shut down to prevent damage from the EMP.

The gamma-ray laser's impact had created a plasma cloud, causing severe electromagnetic interference throughout the surrounding area. Shinji had lost contact with the command center, his telemetry systems, and Eva-02. Even his laser circuit had been knocked out, and Shinji could no longer track where Rei Quatre was.

But then her voice came to him from somewhere above.

《Don't speak kindly to me when you don't mean it.》

Her Eva was directly overhead and closing fast. The giant had plunged into the troposphere, the air around it distorted.

"What...?" Shinji whispered.

Did Ayanami do that? Did Quatre attack us?!

Electrical interference passed into the plug's LCL, and Shinji grimaced in pain. "What are you doing?" His voice cracked.

《You chose her and ruined the Human Instrumentality Project.》

Shinji was confused.

But he still needed to catch Quatre.

It wasn't really a conscious decision. Instead of escape, his confusion led him to continue the task he'd been undertaking before the situation changed. If anything, Shinji had avoided making a decision.

"You're Ayanami, aren't you?"

Before her gamma-ray laser cannon could recharge, Eva-01 created a bright, distinct A.T. Field and pushed it toward the falling Eva-0.0.

"It's not a lie! I'm going to catch you, Ayanami!"

The shock wave slammed into Eva-01 from above. Shinji grunted, and he and his Eva reeled. The sound of the impact carried for kilometers in all directions.

But that was just the wave generated by the Series-0.0's initial descent. When Shinji and Asuka had slowed the falling Eva, the shock wave had kept going at the same speed, spreading and at-tenuating in the atmosphere. Like the foreshock of an earthquake, this impact only signaled the imminent arrival of the real danger.

Somehow, Shinji managed to keep his Eva's feet on the ground.

Then he heard Ayanami's voice again.

《As I change over time, you feel more repelled by me, and you grow more distant... Because with each day, I become more like your mother.》

Her words sparked understanding within Shinji. *Is that why?*

Over the past three years, Shinji had gained the trust of Misato and his other colleagues. His responsibilities had increased, and with them came a sense of satisfaction. He and Asuka were work-ing well together, and—maybe, Shinji thought—getting along. His school life was almost unnaturally normal, and he even had fun sometimes when he made the effort.

But something still unsettled him, and the feeling grew stronger with each passing day. It had come from so deep inside him that he hadn't been able to clearly identify it, but now he understood the source of that unease.

Is that why?

Shinji quickly rejected the thought. "That's not true!"

He had to deny it—to Ayanami and to himself. His cheeks were burning.

《You were only able to perceive me as someone different from your mother until three years ago, when my body was that of a fourteen-year-old.》

"Shut up!"

He trembled as her words stripped his feelings bare.

《If I became exactly like your mother, would you be able to acknowledge me then?》

"Shut up!"

Why is this happening?

Why was Quatre's Eva falling? Why was Quatre saying these things?

Shinji sent out a silent plea for all of this to stop.

The Eva-0.0's and Eva-01's fields collided in midair. Neither gave way to the other, and where they met, a two-dimensional explosion split the sky. What happened in the next moment was not Shinji's conscious plan but a manifestation of his will.

Shinji created a spherical A.T. Field centered on himself. He expanded the field to several dozen times its original size, swallowing everything around him, including Ayanami Quatre's Eva. The air inside the field lost pressure, like a piston pulled from a cylinder. There came a flash of bright white as the field expelled thousands of cubic meters of the lake's water in the shape of a bowl 1,200 meters high. The water was stripped of its heat and instantaneously froze.

Astonishingly, this parabolic dish of ice not only caught the plummeting Eva-0.0 but also the conical, destructive shock wave that spread out around it. As the Eva and its shock wave slammed into the ice, a thin cloud erupted skyward and faded away.

The vast, towering ice sculpture momentarily swelled before crumbling.

From Tokyo-3, the bowl of ice, far taller than the surrounding mountains, seemed to have exploded—except in unnaturally slow motion due to its tremendous scale. The fracturing ice absorbed the last of the shock wave's energy, which otherwise would have slammed into the city. Having lost its spearhead, the wave dissipated, radiating outward and pushing aside all of the clouds in the caldera.

The temperature dropped sharply in the area surrounding Lake Ashi, and glittering diamond dust scattered across the land.

Ibuki Maya, the chief of the science and engineering departments, was inside her Nerv HQ lab along with her team, remotely monitoring data from sensors in the floating deck, which had escaped destruction.

"Send this to the command center," Maya ordered.

The engineers and scientists chatted among themselves excitedly.

"The temperature in the center has fallen from 1,000 degrees Celsius to minus 200. Are we seeing adiabatic cooling?"

"I think there's more to it than that. This sample is showing signs of manipulation of the particles' center of mass."

"Are you talking about controlling the movement of atoms, like with optical tweezers?"

"The electromagnetic interference is completely gone, and the background noise is unusually quiet."

"He's put a stop to all movement," Maya said.

Wearing thin-rimmed glasses and a subdued expression, Maya showed little trace of the cheerful but fastidious woman she'd once been. She now more closely resembled Dr. Akagi Ritsuko, who had, at one time, evoked Maya's trust and scorn alike.

"The chemical bonds of the water molecules in this ice are unusual," Maya remarked.

"With those bonds," one of the scientists said, "the ice is going to be a lot stronger, and with this density...I don't think it will melt easily."

When it came to Evangelions and Angels, solving one mystery often only raised new ones. Over time, the roles of Nerv's engineers and scientists began to overlap in unexpected ways, and both teams were now regularly working in tandem.

As their current chief officer, Maya had inherited stewardship of Nerv Japan's Eva-related technologies, which she continued to develop. Due to the heavy pressure of her duties, Maya rarely smiled anymore. Today, a stern expression wrinkled her brow.

"Unit One is the only Eva to have absorbed an S^2 Engine by itself," she said. "And yet, the past three years have given us little data on it. There was already so much we didn't understand about that Eva, so we can't say if this is a new development or something preexisting."

NEON GENESIS EVANGELION ANIMA

CHAPTER 4

SECOND INVASION

THE EVENING CONTINUED to darken, and the combination of diamond dust and densely rising fog blocked what little visibility remained. The shock wave's impact had knocked Eva-01 back, but it hadn't fallen into the lake. As ice shards continued to fall, Shinji's Eva stood on the frozen surface of Lake Ashi.

Shinji was out of breath, his heart pounding. The flood of endorphins made him feel like he might puke. The sensors in his plugsuit detected his agitation. Shinji felt a small jolt of pain in his arm, and his eyebrows twitched. A soft resin needle had delivered a sedative straight into his veins.

"What...happened?" Shinji panted.
The world around him had become frozen and white.
Eva-01 did this.

What happened to Quatre...and her Eva-0.0?
"I told you to shut up."

He'd acted out of embarrassment, wanting to silence her words.

What have I done?

A loud rumble broke the stillness.

A mountain of fallen ice blasted into the air. An arm thrust out, striking the frozen surface of the lake as Quatre's Eva leaped up and rushed toward Eva-01, grasping the giant with one bare hand.

"Ayanami! Number Quatre!"

Number Quatre, he'd said—not as a name, but as the number she'd been assigned. Misato detested that practice—*Don't treat a human being like she's a number*, she'd said—and Shinji felt the same way, or at least, he'd thought he did. But in the moment, on a subconscious level, he'd used the number to separate her from the other Ayanamis. This one was broken.

Her Eva was severely damaged. It had lost its shoulder sensor arrays and propellant system, and its body was misshapen—more so than the impact should have caused.

An Eva's shape is determined by its pilot's self-identity...

The twisted and mangled Eva-0.0 dragged its broken laser cannon in its right hand, attacking Eva-01 with its left.

Taken aback by this vicious tenacity, Shinji reflexively asked, "Do you want to kill me, Number Quatre?!"

The reply came by speaker. It was Quatre's voice.

《Quatre doesn't want to kill you. *Ayanami* does.》

Meaning the girl Shinji's mind attached the name *Ayanami* to—the one in the high-school uniform. The melancholy Trois.

"That...can't be!"

《If this is the world you wanted, Ikari-kun, then maybe if I kill you...》

She left the rest unsaid.

What does she think will happen?

Dropping its A.T. Field and tucking into a roll, Eva-01 nimbly slid across the ice, maneuvering behind the other Eva.

Quatre's voice sounded tearful. 《After all, this world is already ending.》

Shinji didn't know what she meant, but her words inexplicably pierced him.

Had that last part come from Ayanami?

"I don't understand what you're saying!"

If Shinji could disconnect the Series-0.0 Eva's external S^2 Engine, its internal power would quickly run out, and the giant would be immobilized. At least, that was Shinji's plan.

What?!

The S^2 Engine was supposed to have been hooked up to the rear-facing umbilical connector, but Quatre's engine had fused directly into the Eva's back.

Asuka's Eva-02 crawled from the rubble of the annihilated sniping post at Mount Komagatake. The power source indicator on her entry plug's display flickered between the remote supply and the Eva's internal reserves.

"Tch. There must be a malfunction somewhere."

It's a miracle the umbilical cable wasn't severed completely.

Wait—why is everything white?!

She'd heard and felt a tremendous rumbling, but the blast had severed her data link, leaving her in the dark about what had happened.

The floor jolted and sunk a little, and Eva-02's power source switched to internal reserves. The operational time limit began its frantic countdown.

Well... now *my umbilical cable is severed. Some part of the structure beneath me, weakened from the blast, must have given way.*

I need to get out of here fast...

When she emerged from the scorched, crumbling building, the first thing she saw was the two Evas battling on the frozen white lake.

But then she saw something else.

"What?"

The vision was straight out of a nightmare.

As ice crystals cascaded down, a dense fog rose from Lake Ashi's frozen surface like steam from a boiling pot.

The Eva-0.0 and Eva-01 grappled with each other.

Then, for an instant, the fog parted, and Asuka saw a third giant figure striding across the ice, away from the tussling pair and toward Tokyo-3.

Where had that one come from?

"It can't be," she gasped. "Shinji!"

The giant figure was so shocking that briefly her vision and hearing distorted. When she called Shinji's name, she felt as if she were struggling against a great weight.

The electromagnetic interference had disappeared, and Eva-02's communication systems finished rebooting. From the command center, Misato's voice reverberated in the plug's LCL.

《Follow the anti-Angel counterattack sequence. Ready the city's defenses. The target is...Unit Quatre!》

Everyone was focused on Quatre's Eva.

But it was the other giant, the one with the familiar, shark-like face, that made Asuka start shouting.

"Shinji! A mass-production Eva is here! Behind you!"

Ice crystals flitted through the air as far as she could see, and for a moment, Asuka wondered if the sparkling light had tricked her into seeing a phantom. But no, the white giant really was there.

"Command center, this is an emergency! There's a mass-production Eva directly between you and Unit One! Why haven't you noticed?!"

"What did she say?!" Misato yelled.

On a normal day, the middle of Lake Ashi was easily visible from Tokyo-3, but Nerv's line of sight, and its electronic sensors, were blocked by the still-collapsing mountains of ice and the rising white fog.

The cameras at Mount Komagatake had been destroyed, and the camera at Yamabushi Pass on the western shore was aimed at Eva-01 and the Series-0.0 Eva. But when this camera panned to the left, the image of the white giant sent a shock wave of its own through the command center.

A wiper arm passed across the camera lens, clearing away the condensation. For a moment, the rising clouds parted, and the creature could be seen lumbering toward the city. Its head rose above the fog, but the rest of its massive body remained shrouded.

Misato started barking orders. "As of this moment, our objective is to annihilate that mass-production Eva! Notify the UN and government officials! If Unit Quatre interferes, disable it by any means necessary!"

Throughout Tokyo-3, the alarm systems switched from disaster to combat.

It's finally come, Misato thought, *but...*

The commander called Maya's lab on the main screen. "What's the status of the other two orbital Evas?"

"Their synchrographs are an absolute mess," Maya said. "According to our simulations, if they activate now, there's a ninety-six percent chance they'll go berserk. Where's Trois? She needs to control them...or else."

Aoba answered. "The security team brought her to the public shelter in sector twelve. We haven't heard from them since."

My precious search-and-destroy system is unusable!

"We don't have anything that can fight it," Misato said. "We need to hurry and—"

Hyuga interrupted, his voice uncertain. "What's happening? I'm not getting a color pattern!"

It took Misato a moment to absorb what he'd said. "—prepare the armament transport—Wait, what does that mean?"

"We stored the individual DNA patterns of all the mass-production Evangelions in our databanks, but I'm not getting a match with any of the patterns we encountered three years ago."

Every member of Nerv Japan had been searching for Seele's vanished Evas, but none of them had expected one to appear without warning...and so close to home.

The giant had come from nowhere, as if rising out of the frozen fog, a monster striding across the ice, indifferent to the events happening around it.

"That's impossible!" Shinji shouted angrily back at Asuka.

But his restored data link gave him coordinates and an image, hazy through the showering ice crystals, of the white giant.

This can't be happening.

If that's the mass-production Eva's current position, the thing must have walked right past me. I should have noticed!

Shinji looked back and forth between the mass-production Eva on his display and the Series-0.0 Eva in front of him.

He grunted as he blocked Eva-0.0's punch with Eva-01's arm, which recoiled upward, leaving his front undefended.

During their fight, Quatre's Eva had only been attacking with its left arm, its right hand still clinging to the massive laser cannon. The entire right arm seemed to have been damaged from the shoulder down.

But now, seizing Shinji's moment of weakness, the arm moved and—

—shattered like so much glass.

"Was it frozen?"

Eva-0.0 collapsed onto the ice, sheltering its shattered arm beneath its body. A plume of ice dust rose and scattered.

The pain from the feedback must have been intolerable. The fallen Eva writhed on the ground, its feet scraping nosily against the ice.

Rei Quatre's anguished cry echoed through the Eva's speakers.

"Ayanami—Quatre! Don't move!"

Her wailing was more than he could bear. Shinji turned his attention to the mass-production Eva. Easier to deal with that monster than face a friend in pain.

Eva-01 turned and vanished into the thick, cold fog.

《Command, this is Asuka. Send me a weapon! Everything at the sniping post has been melted!》

Asuka's voice sounded distant through the hydrospeaker in Shinji's entry plug.

The response didn't please her. 《We can't do that. The underground rail system is damaged south of Togendai.》

《Damn it! Well, as long as the tunnel hasn't collapsed, I can run through it on my own. There's an exit in Togendai. I can arm myself and get back outside. I want a positron rifle! I don't have much power left. Shinji, say something!》

Shinji winced. When he replied, his words tumbled out reluctantly, as if he were making an excuse.

"Eva-0.0 is disabled on the ice...I think. I'm running across the lake to get in front of the mass-production Eva. My Type-F has internal weapons—I'll try to stop it."

Eva-02 dove into the shaft of the broken elevator.

Meanwhile, at an anti-air station not far from the sniping post, every automated artillery cannon that could aim below the horizon swiveled in unison and engaged the mass-production Eva. But the extremely low temperature robbed the barrels' special steel of its strength. The motors lost conductivity and couldn't operate smoothly. Several cannons exploded.

《Shinji-kun?》 Misato's voice. 《We're sending up additional armaments with Asuka at Togendai. Regroup with her there. I know we've been trying to find one of these white giant bastards, but if we don't do this properly, the result could be catastrophic!》

Eva-01 ran through the crystalline mists of Lake Ashi as if fleeing from Rei Quatre. Soon, his Eva overtook the white giant in the haze. After three years, he'd finally found the enemy.

Where did its wings go? And why are its bones sticking out?

"Confirming visual on the mass-production Eva. It's holding a staff-like weapon."

The enemy kept on walking, as if it had a purpose.

Guided munitions from the city's defense sectors soared over the mountains of ice to join the direct attacks from the anti-air station. But their ordnance didn't pack enough punch to slow the mass-production Eva's silent strides.

"Its A.T. Field is blocking the attacks!" Shinji said.

He opened the front-facing armor plates on his Eva's shoulder pylons. Using the icy mist as cover, he closed in on the mass-production Eva and fired two impact bolts.

The command center was a flurry of activity.

"Defense systems, cease fire!"

"Shinji-kun, what the hell are you doing?" Misato shouted. "Don't rush into the targeting area!"

《I need to buy you some time. It's approaching the city!》

"Get a hold of yourself!" Misato examined Eva-01's images of the mass-production Eva.

Something about this monster looks different from before. She called Maya in the laboratory.

"Are you seeing this? Tell me what you think."

《If its form has changed, then we should assume that its tactics and fighting abilities have also changed in the last three years.》

A blindingly bright flash filled the command center's main screen.

Eva-01 had fired its impact bolts, which were close-range projectile weapons unique, for now, to the Type-F Evas. In front of each shoulder pylon floated a small black orb, a virtual image created by the phase interaction of the A.T. Field and normal space. But the surge of electricity—a product of the difference in potential—was real, and several whip-like bolts of lightning slammed into the target. Still—

"No effect," Misato said. "Is it because of the enemy's A.T. Field? Run the pattern analysis again!"

"Still no match!" Hyuga said. "No color pattern."

"Could its shield be something other than an A.T. Field?"

From the laboratory, Maya offered, "If there's no pattern, maybe that means the mass-production Eva isn't alive. It's an animated corpse."

The mass-production Evas had been killed by Eva-01 in the Battle at Nerv HQ three years prior. Most of their corpses had disappeared before they could be recovered.

"If that thing is dead," Misato said, "then how is it getting power? How is it manifesting a shield? Maybe that cocoon inside its ribcage is its core."

《Maybe.》 Maya paused. 《We don't know a single thing about the cocoon. It could be anything.》

"Pattern detected! It's blue!" Hyuga shouted, and Shinji yelped.

"What?!" Misato looked up from her terminal.

On the main screen, the mass-production Eva's cocoon cracked open. An arm emerged and threw a javelin made of light. Eva-01 raised its left arm to protect its face, and the spear pierced its metal plating.

I know that arm!

Eva-01's restraint armor shattered where it had been struck, and sharp, agonizing feedback flooded Shinji. But despite the pain, his mind made the connection.

"That's the arm of the Angel Sachiel!"

He would have recognized it anywhere. After all, it was the first Angel he'd faced.

"How and why is an Angel coming out of that cocoon?!"

Eva-01 hopped backward and retrieved a progressive knife from its shoulder pylon. The knife was larger, its blade thicker, than the one it had replaced. It was shaped something like a mountaineer's machete. The high-frequency vibrations of its blade turned the ice crystals that landed on it into wisps of steam.

Shinji swung his prog knife. The blade's tip struck the mass-production Eva's power shield and went no further.

The mass-production Eva, carrying its cocoon and the Angel within, continued walking in silence. Its one strike had come from Sachiel's arm. No attack came from the giant itself.

《Shinji-kun,》 Hyuga said, 《don't provoke it needlessly.》

"Keep collecting data," Shinji said. "We need to find a weakness!"

Is there nothing else I can try?

The monster's shield had stopped both the impact bolts and the prog knife.

But wait—

Eva-01 opened the front panel of its shoulder pylons and prepared to fire another round of impact bolts. The two black spheres materialized again, but this time, they didn't generate lightning. Instead, they remained in place while Shinji rushed forward and crashed them through the mass-production Eva's shield.

The floating spheres had been designed to create an intensely powerful difference in electrical potential. They worked by focusing an A.T. Field large enough to shield the Eva's entire body into two single points. Each had a heightened phase differential with the space around it.

And now Shinji was smashing them directly into his enemy.

"I'll tear through you!" he shouted.

And he did. The black spheres tore through the enemy's shield, and Eva-01 pushed its shoulder through the hole. The next instant, Sachiel's arm came flying out to counterattack—but Shinji was expecting it.

Come on, that arm is longer than the cocoon is wide. How the hell does it fit inside there?

Sachiel's hand flicked open, and a javelin extended out, piercing Eva-01's arm. Shinji gritted his teeth against the pain, grabbed the Angel's arm, and growled, "Come on out!"

Shinji yanked the Angel from its cocoon with all his strength. He could feel something tearing on the other side. When the arm emerged, Shinji could see that its other end was attached to a small, soft, larva-like body, which still clung to the cocoon.

"It's not fully formed yet..."

Shinji felt eyes upon him. The mass-production Eva turned its head and looked at him for the first time.

The cocoon's carrier—*Mother?* Shinji wondered—swung its arm and struck Eva-01 with its staff. Shinji and his Eva went flying.

He screamed in pain.

The single strike had broken Eva-01's arm, and the giant crashed into the ice, bouncing to a stop.

But the hand that had been holding the prog knife was empty.

The blade stuck from the cocoon where Shinji believed Sachiel's core to be. He'd sunk it deep.

"How's that?" Shinji shouted.

The knife had struck true. The Angel's body began to disintegrate from the edges in.

"I did it!"

Cheers filled the command center, but the mass-production Eva didn't falter in its approach.

Scattering tiny fragments of the disintegrating Sachiel through the cleft in its cocoon, the giant changed course, proceeding toward a new goal.

"Or did I?"

Shinji had guessed—wrongly, it appeared—that the stillborn Angel in that cocoon had been providing power to, and maintaining control over, the animated corpse of the mass-production Eva.

A wall of ice blocked the mass-production Eva's path ahead. The shock wave from the heavens had shattered more than half of the ice bowl Eva-01 had created in its temporary berserk state, but the remaining ice formed a thick-walled dam across the valley, with Tokyo-3 sheltered on the far side.

I'll attack again when the mass-production Eva stops at the wall!

But Shinji never got the chance. The Eva didn't stop. It passed straight into the ice.

"What?"

The monster didn't break or melt the ice. Nothing shattered. The giant simply...disappeared into the wall, as if becoming one with it.

Shinji was stunned.

"I can't let it escape!"

He brought his Eva to its feet. As he did, the restraint armor split open and fell off its shoulder, perhaps due to the impact that had broken its arm.

Unconcerned, Shinji pursued the white giant with his damaged Eva.

He opened the remaining shoulder pylon and fired a volley of impact bolts, but the severely low temperature impeded the air's conductivity, and the bolts went wild, striking the ice wall instead. The mass-production Eva finished submerging into the ice and vanished.

A moment too late, Eva-01 collided with the ice wall in an explosion far larger than the giant itself. But it didn't reach the enemy.

Shinji drew his other progressive knife and thrust it into the ice. Each time he struck, the vibrations created a wide burst of shards, but Shinji never felt the blade strike the flesh he sought.

"Command! I've lost the mass-production Eva. I don't know what happened."

《Shinji, find a way to cross that ice wall. The longer you delay, the later you'll join Asuka. How's your right arm?》

"Broken, but we can still fight."

Damn it!

Eva-01 pounded the ice with its good arm. Nothing unusual was supposed to happen today. He should be having dinner with Asuka and Misato-san right now.

"Damn it! What the hell is going on?!"

《This is the world you chose, Ikari-kun.》

The ice clouds parted behind Eva-01, revealing the Series-0.0 Eva standing there like a ghost.

"Quatre?!"

Her Eva was changing shape; its metal shrieked and groaned. Its body was stiffening. *Has it gone berserk?*

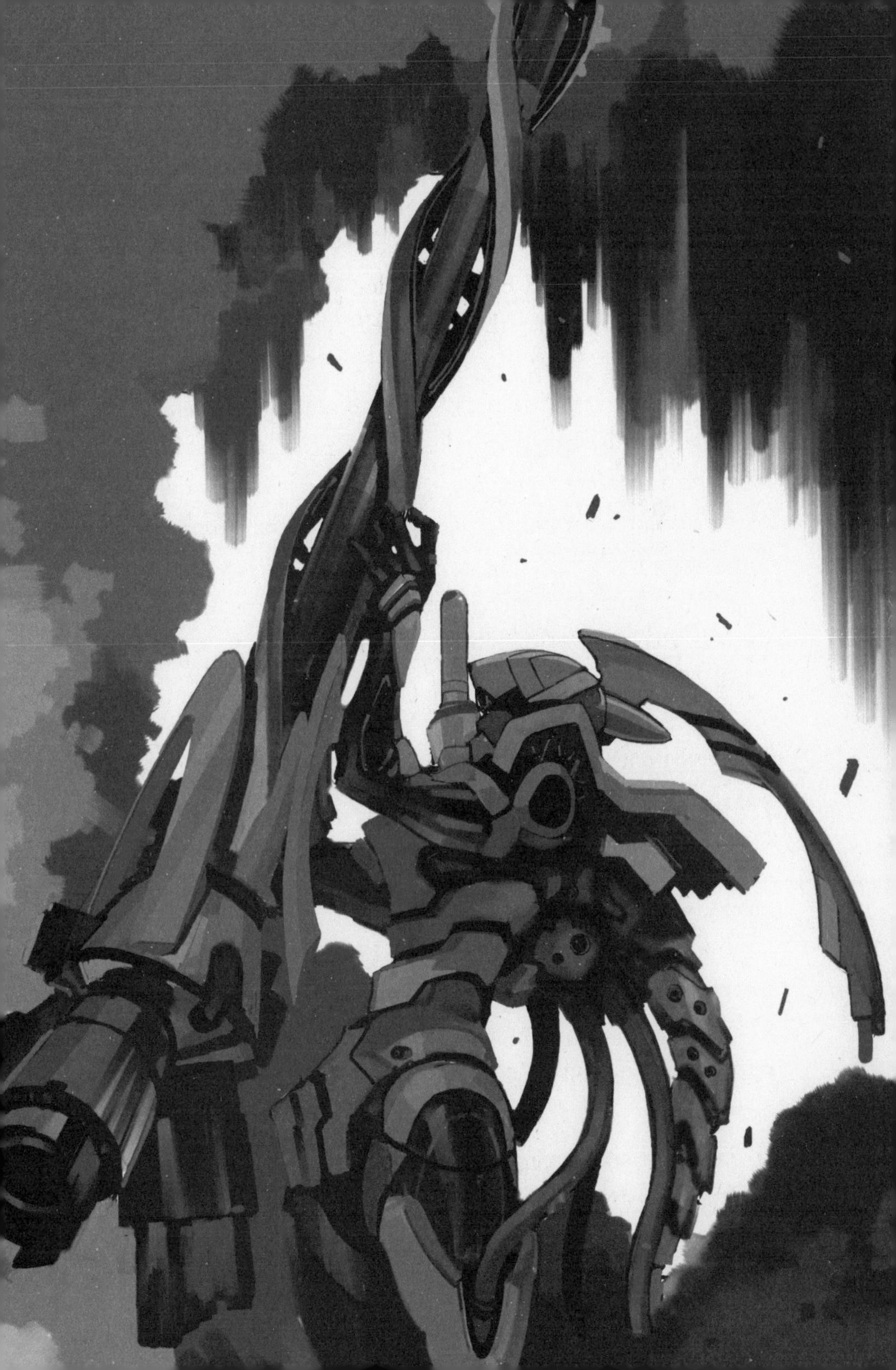

And there was the gamma-ray laser cannon—*fused directly to its upper arm.*

The launch rail had twisted unnaturally to point directly at Shinji.

Nothing unusual was supposed to happen today.

I was going to check my e-mail, watch a movie, and go to bed. That was supposed to be it.

Eva-01 dodged backward.

But the cannon's tip followed and pressed against his outer armor with a distant thud.

《Save me. Take me back to that time.》

The nuclear excitement unit is damaged, so there's no way it can fire—

This was the last thought of Ikari Shinji in his final moments as a living human being.

With a six-inch diameter and four hundred megaelectron-volts of energy, the gamma-ray laser was a dazzling golden light capable of piercing through anything.

The fierce beam punched through Eva-01's armor like paper, entered the giant through its side, sliced a notch out of its core and S^2 Engine, evaporated the entry plug whole, and exited through the back of the neck, hurtling into the heavens.

CHAPTER 5

INTO HELL

ASUKA, IN EVA-02, ran through the underground tunnels, unaware that Shinji and Eva-01 had been destroyed.

The weapons had been waiting for her at the end of the broken rail line. Because her Eva's IFF system had been taken offline by the electromagnetic interference, syncing the positron rifle's FCS had cost her a little extra time, but she'd also equipped herself with a Powered 8—a next-gen revision of the pallet gun—and two curved swords.

Mere paces from the exit to Togendai, Asuka froze. Eva-02 was towing a mobile power terminal on a linear transport rail. The rail cart sensed that the Eva had stopped but wasn't capable of halting its momentum nearly as quickly. Sparks sprayed from the cart's wheels as it struggled to brake. Asuka planted a foot in front of the vehicle to stop it.

"Misato," Asuka said. "Misato! Can you tell me what's going on? I've got a mass-production Eva down here!"

Like Nerv's previous HQ, the new headquarters had been

built atop several dozen layers of thick armor. Unlike the old construction, the new foundation contained small gaps between each of the layers, spaced wider apart the deeper they went. The concept was the same as spaced armor on a tank; the plating absorbed and dispersed the force of incoming attacks, the gaps leaving room for any residual force to dissipate before reaching the next layer.

Through one such gap walked a white giant, its head narrowly avoiding wedging itself in the various divots formed by the angular ceiling.

Asuka transmitted the mass-production Eva's coordinates along with a video feed to the command center. The other end of the line erupted in a flurry of crosstalk. Misato sounded surprised as she said, 《Wait... Asuka? Is this real? How could it have gotten inside?》

It was the same mutated mass-production Eva that Shinji had failed to finish off. The larval Angel Sachiel, still mid-disintegration, dangled from its broken cocoon as the giant walked. Walking toward—

"The old HQ!" Asuka said.

Why, though? What is its goal?

《Asuka, listen to me. I'm going to unseal the Lance of Longinus. Come retrieve it.》

Misato must have a bad feeling about this... She doesn't want me fighting that thing—she wants me to finish it off in a single strike. In an earlier time, she'd said, *All we need are me and Unit-02.* The memory made her chuckle.

《What's funny?》

"Nothing. Unit Two, acknowledged. Misato, where's Shinji?"

《We don't know the situation on the lake. There's been another burst of electromagnetic interference. I suspect Quatre is still operational and has fired her laser again, but we've lost contact with Unit One. I've just launched a drone, so I'll have a better idea soon.》

What the heck are you doing, Super Shinji?

Misato put her hands on her hips, surveying the command center.

"You were after the inner citadel the whole time," she muttered.

Reports from every emergency shelter converged; the extremely low temperatures had caused superconductive interference that halted power transmission in affected areas, water pipes were freezing and bursting—in some places causing floods—and the water was entering other cracks, freezing, and causing a chain reaction of damage.

But it was even colder outdoors. Merely breathing the air was potentially fatal. If a catastrophe occurred beneath the surface, how could the residents possibly be evacuated from the caldera?

"Forget about fielding complaints for the moment. Asuka and Unit Two need our full support. Understood?"

The command room responded in agreement.

Asuka stood at the door to Underground Armory Six, or as Misato had named it, Pandora's Box. At the time, the Eva pilots hadn't been amused, but Kaji had said, "We can't go around saying this is where we're storing the Lance of Longinus, can we?" So, the name had stuck.

The armory had been sealed behind a series of blast doors, which had all been remotely unlocked from the command center except for the last one.

Asuka grumbled. "I told you my IFF system wasn't working."

She manually entered her backup identification code, and the lock disengaged. The sound of a vacuum pump stopped.

The Lance of Longinus slowly rose from the vessel of liquid nitrogen in which it had been stored. Eva-02's right hand grasped the weapon.

Ugh...

"How disgusting."

Even near absolute zero, it's still humming.

The lance vibrated just at the edge of perceptibility.

Apparently, the original one had, too. Three years ago, Eva-00 had thrown the lance at Arael, and the weapon had landed on the moon, where it remained to this day.

And this is a copy.

This particular weapon held a deeper significance for Asuka. In the final stage of the Human Instrumentality Project, this lance had pierced through her and Eva-02.

"This must be fate," she said under her breath. She furrowed her brow.

But what the hell is fate?

A mass-production Eva had carried the lance into the Battle at Nerv HQ. Supposedly, the weapon was a copy of the original, but Asuka had trouble conceiving how Seele could possibly have managed to replicate the weapon.

Evangelions themselves relied on a framework of extraordinary technology, but they could still be understood as the product of advancements in science made by the minds and efforts of humankind. Replicating the lance, on the other hand, should have been far too great a leap.

As the mass-production Eva continued its march, the path ahead opened up. The low ceiling—low to a giant, anyway—gradually raised, and the space between the rows of support pillars widened. The stark cleanliness of bare concrete transitioned into the decay of an abandoned ruin. Each step the white giant took stirred up fresh clouds of ash-colored dust.

The Eva had reached the outer edge of the old Geofront.

The destruction was left over from the Battle at Nerv HQ, when the swarm of mass-production Evas had descended upon the Geofront and dropped the ceiling and its city into the underground, where the wreckage remained untouched for three years. The Geofront had been abandoned in favor of sealing away the former HQ at its center.

An unadorned wall of Hard Tektite Concrete interrupted the scene of devastation. When viewed from below, the rubble obscured the structure's full scope, but the barrier surrounding the former HQ formed a giant dome—or, as most people called it, a sarcophagus—over the top of it. An opening in the Geofront's ceiling provided a partial view from above ground, though the sarcophagus was too large to be seen all at once.

And on the inside...

The ground exploded beneath the mass-production Eva, the floor giving way and sucking the giant under.

The Eva remained perfectly upright as it landed on the level below.

The very next moment, even as dust was still thick in the air, the Lance of Longinus impaled the giant through its chin, sticking out the back of its head.

Standing before the white monster, Eva-02's eyes glimmered through the smoke of the explosion.

"I know it's been a while since we last met," Asuka said as calmly as she could manage. "I'm sorry to ambush you like this."

Eva-02's red-armored arm wrenched the lance upward.

The lance's twin tines were twisted into a double helix that became a single shaft. The small, open space in the middle of the helix began radiating light, and the mass-production Eva's chin disintegrated to dust.

A hole opened up all the way through the back of the Eva's skull, exposing the giant's neckbones to the air. The top of the monster's jaw remained, with its ghoulish row of white teeth. The mass-production Eva staggered, raising its staff aloft, and—

Wham!

The mass-production Eva's power shield materialized, knocking Eva-02 back, but Asuka managed to keep her hold on the lance.

"How are you still moving?! With that cocoon in your chest, I was sure your core would be in your head."

Assuming this monster even has a core.

Eva-02 gripped the lance tighter.

"Come on! In a zombie movie, you always have to go for the head."

The mass-production Eva took one step to regain its balance and then drew its arm back, holding the staff above its shoulder.

What, are you going to throw that at me? You'll never hit me!

But the white giant's target wasn't Eva-02. Even on this lower level, the wall of the sarcophagus remained in sight.

A whoosh of air brushed past Asuka.

The mass-production Eva had thrown its staff like a javelin at the sarcophagus's armored wall.

Watching through their monitors, the command center technicians didn't expect the staff would do more than *maybe* scratch the shell. But the giant had placed a power shield on the staff's tip, and the weapon struck the sarcophagus with terrible force, piercing the outermost layer of Hard Tektite Concrete and sending a sunburst of cracks down into the next layer.

But the sarcophagus held. Or at least, that's what Asuka was thinking when the mass-production Eva charged past Eva-02 toward the wall.

There was a bright light followed by a terrific impact.

"Asuka!" Misato shouted. "Sachiel is still inside the cocoon!"

The light had come from Sachiel's face, which turned to dust as the last of the Angel's power was spent. The cocoon was now empty.

The energy beam stripped away several more layers of HTC, allowing the mass-production Eva to smash through. The wall of the sarcophagus crumbled, and the white giant, now streaked with blood, tumbled inside.

Misato pounded her fist on the commander's console. "Damn it!"

On the main screen, the Magi AI system presented the option of initiating the base's self-destruct sequence and announced that it was considering the merits.

Alarms blared, and red siren lights, located every one hundred meters along the sarcophagus's wall, began to spin. Industrial lights inside the casket switched on, illuminating the ruins of the attack from three years ago. At the center of those ruins was—

A black sphere—like a hole torn from the world.

An eerie, black dome filled the space the former Nerv HQ building had once occupied. It didn't reflect even the slightest light, appearing like a hole neatly ripped in the structure. The dome was merely the top of a sphere, extending below the Geofront's surface, with Lilith—the second Angel and progenitor of humanity—at its center.

Toward the end of the Battle at Nerv HQ, just after Shinji and Eva-01 destroyed the altar of light in the sky and put an end to the Human Instrumentality Project, Lilith had created a pocket of space where time was frozen—this sphere of perfect darkness.

Supposedly, the space contained everyone who had been in or beneath the HQ at the time, including Ikari Gendo, Akagi Ritsuko, 150-odd workers, and a dozen or more soldiers from the SSDF—all of whom had been frozen instantaneously.

No device, exploratory beam, or sound wave had been able to penetrate the sphere. Even its temperature was unmeasurable.

The object had been named the Chronostatic Sphere, though later examination had shown that it was more egg-shaped than spherical. But that was the extent of what anyone had learned about it. The speculation about time being frozen within hadn't come from any direct measurements, as no physical object, electromagnetic wave, or anything—down to and including neutrinos—had been able to penetrate it.

But the complete lack of data was, in itself, informative. A conjecture arose—*nothing propagates though the field because there's no time for anything to propagate*. A counterargument followed, perhaps obvious: *Time can bend, but it can't stop altogether without violating the laws of physics*. The conclusion: *Time is, in effect, frozen—as close to true stasis as temporally possible*.

Those who knew of the sphere held many theories about its nature, and vigorously debated them, but they all agreed on the theory about *why* it had come to be.

When the Human Instrumentality Project was terminated, Lilith went to sleep—an absolute sleep, impossible to disturb.

No one knew the purpose of this slumber or when the second Angel might awaken. Nor did they know what would—or wouldn't—happen when it did. And so a decision was made to seal away the entire Geofront. A few passive sensors had been left behind, but all active investigations into the sphere had been halted.

The victims swallowed by the Chronostatic Sphere were to be treated as if they'd died in the battle. Everyone involved agreed to go along with this story, even if they didn't accept it in their hearts. Three years later, the black sphere remained, swallowing up their thoughts and prayers for the people trapped within.

《Asuka! Stop that Eva!》

And now, a visitor had come.

"Yeah, you don't have to tell me!"

Eva-02 decoupled its umbilical cable with a spray of sparks. Asuka dashed forward as the internal battery timer began racing toward zero.

Asuka didn't know why the mass-production Eva had come here, but she couldn't shake the feeling that something bad was about to happen.

Where is its weak point? Misato thought impatiently. *What's powering it?* She noticed something on the video feed and brought it to Asuka's attention.

《Sachiel may be gone, but there's a red light coming from the rear of the cocoon. Stab it!》

Asuka didn't think that sounded like much of a strategy, but she needed to do *something*.

"On it!"

Asuka swept the mass-production Eva's legs with the lance's shaft. When the giant toppled, she ran ahead of it, positioning herself directly in its field of view. She didn't know what effect the lance would have on the giant. And if the mass-production Eva exploded, she didn't know what effect *that* would have on the Chronostatic Sphere. But whatever might come, she'd hold it back with her Eva's A.T. Field.

As the mass-production Eva rose to its feet, Eva-02 spun to face it, dust thick in the air. Asuka put the momentum of her turn into a fierce thrust with the lance.

The white giant activated its power shield, but the Lance of Longinus pierced through it, sparks flying, toward the glowing spot within the cocoon.

"There!"

The lance met resistance, its twin prongs catching *something* and coming out the enemy's back.

In that moment, Asuka knew, as if the lance had spoken to her, *This is what gave life to this corpse.*

The white giant tried to push Eva-02 away, but Asuka smoothly ducked the attack. Keeping her hands on the lance, she came up on the other side of the shaft, like a gymnast switching sides under a horizontal bar. She threw her Eva's full weight against her enemy and drove the lance deeper.

The mass-production Eva grabbed Eva-02's mask from behind, but it was too late.

"Go back to being dead," she said.

The lance trembled, and the helix at the base of its prongs expanded and glowed.

The *thing* at the back of the cocoon shattered, and the five white fingers obstructing the view through her holographic display began to disintegrate as if the tissue were unraveling.

Then the rest of the mass-production Eva's body followed.

It's over.

But when Asuka glanced over her shoulder, the decaying giant wasn't looking at her. Its eyes were fixed on the blackness of the Chronostatic Sphere.

And in its face, Asuka saw satisfaction.

The towering monster fell to the ground with a thunderous crash, and the shrine of the giant black egg returned to silence.

《Good work, Asuka. Leave the cleanup to us.》Misato's voice was unexpectedly dispirited. 《I hate to ask anything more of you, but as quickly as you can, take the nearest elevator back to the surface. Unit One was disabled in combat, and I need you to assist with the emergency recovery.》

"Shinji? What did that idiot do?"

By the time anyone at Nerv learned that Eva-01 had been damaged beyond the point of return, Ayanami Quatre and her Series-0.0 Eva had disappeared from the battlefield.

Misato convened a search, but no trace of Quatre could be found. It was as if she'd been erased.

NEON GENESIS
EVANGELION ANIMA

CHAPTER 6

THE WHITE HERALD

T HE TEMPERATURE INSIDE the caldera had risen considerably, though it was still below freezing.

Repairs on Tokyo-3 quickly ran aground.

Voltage drops due to the low temperatures left the electric
trains largely inoperable. Fortunately, the work crews managed
to get the internal combustion engines running again, but once
turned off, the engines weren't easily restarted, which meant the
trains had to run nonstop.

Construction noise might have been a nuisance, but the snow
absorbed much of the sound. Even from a short distance, the
work sites looked almost like mirages.

Snow.

The ice shards attracted moisture from the air and caused
snow to fall inside the caldera, much to the bewilderment of the
citizens eager to get their city working again.

For the past twenty-five years, no one in Japan had seen snow.

It was after sunset now, but the rising cold mists lent a soft glow to the sky above Tokyo-3. From the perspective of the patrolling drones, which managed to stay in flight despite the flurries accumulating on their frames, the Hakone caldera looked just like a snow globe.

Three black, bulletproof, security-division SUVs traveled the snowy roads with trepidation. Upon arrival at Nerv HQ, the middle vehicle's door slid open, revealing Ayanami Trois sitting in a wheelchair.

She didn't yet know that Ayanami Quatre—or in a sense, she herself—had attacked Shinji and vanished, and she didn't understand why her hands and feet had been placed in restraints.

Something white landed on her shackles.

"It's cold," she said.

Still in a haze, unable to hear the voices of her other selves, Ayanami Rei noticed the white substance falling all around her.

Flower petals? No, these are melting.

Japan didn't have winters anymore.

Ayanami Rei Trois gazed into the monotone world of Eva-01's creation, seeing snow for the first time.

I want to fall asleep just like this, surrounded by white.

PART 2

NEON GENESIS

NATIVITY

EVANGELION: ANIMA

NEON GENESIS
EVANGELION ANIMA

CHAPTER 7

EXTINCTION PROTOCOL

AFTER SHOOTING SHINJI, Ayanami Rei Quatre vanished into the haze, leaving no emissions trail, no footprints, no trace at all.

Through mental mirroring, the clone was supposed to have been under the control of Rei Trois—the primary Rei, the one with the soul.

Trois was immediately suspected of having instigated Quatre's rebellion, whether intentionally or through negligence, and she was now undergoing intense questioning by the intelligence division.

But her interrogators' voices sounded distant and hollow, as if a wall separated them from her. And Cinq and Six's voices had gone silent as well.

The feeling was less like losing her sisters and more like losing a part of her body. She shut herself away inside.

Asuka was the first to visit Rei during her captivity, opening the door with a barrage of furious shouting and plowing through the interrogators' attempts to block her entry. Once inside, she spat a single, anguished question.

"Why?"

In that moment, Rei Trois realized that the interrogators had been telling the truth; Rei Quatre, her other self, had shot and killed Shinji.

Even now, Ayanami's face remained as inscrutable as it had been three years ago, but Asuka saw that Trois hadn't purposefully made Quatre go berserk. Still, knowing Rei's intentions, or lack thereof, didn't change what had happened.

Asuka grabbed Ayanami by the collar of her school uniform and pulled her to her feet.

"Don't give up so easily," Asuka said. "Shinji can't die when I still owe him for saving me three years ago."

Asuka had dragged Eva-01 back to Nerv HQ, where the fallen giant was placed not into the primary hangar, Cage One, but Cage Two, which had long been sealed off. The cage had been kept as a backup and was located in what was now the oldest section of the complex, just beyond the northern outskirts of the Geofront. Its roof had collapsed in the Battle at Nerv HQ, and the hangar remained open to the air. It was also where the mass-production Evas had been disassembled.

Scans of Eva-01's internals perplexed both the engineering and science teams. They'd hoped to determine whether Shinji was dead or alive but instead saw something entirely beyond their understanding.

Not only was there no sign of Shinji or the entry plug, but the physical boundaries between the internal components of the giant's body—its skeletal structure, organs, muscles—had blurred, and the components now appeared to be mixing together. Not believing their eyes, the engineers in the old control booth brushed the dust off their display screens, but what they saw grew no clearer.

The gamma-ray laser had melted through Eva-01's restraint armor. At the beam's entry and exit points, the metal plating rippled out like the surface of a lake after a large rock has been hurled into it. The insides were a mess, burned all through. Some parts had instantly evaporated or exploded. But the damage explained only some of what the engineers found in the scans. The boundaries between all of the Eva's internals—even its skeleton—were becoming indistinct. The work crew had had to scramble to fill the long-neglected cage with LCL before the 3,600-ton Eva collapsed under its own weight.

The giant humanoid housed inside the Type-F restraint armor appeared to be turning into a soup, a blank slate with no connection to what it had once been...with one exception. While the body died away, one component continued to produce dangerous levels of energy.

The S^2 Engine.

This power plant was a combination of the Eva's own core and an engine that had once belonged to the Angel Zeruel, whose body the Eva had consumed in a berserk state. It freed Eva-01 from its reliance on the power cables, but it was more than just an engine; it was the beating heart that allowed for the Eva's continued existence.

And now the engine was highly unstable, putting out berserk-level power in irregular bursts before dropping back to normal levels. The giant rumbled like a distant earthquake.

Whether Shinji was alive or dead—if he even existed anymore—any attempts to recover him had to be set aside. The top priority was stopping the volatile S^2 Engine. If left unchecked, its sudden release of energy could trigger a cataclysmic Third Impact.

The S^2 Engine was a cauldron ready to boil over, and the engineers and scientists needed to find some way to gain control over it, release its energy safely—but not too fast—and deliver Eva-01 to a gentle death.

The team had just resigned themselves to this bitter mission when the situation grew worse.

With dread, Maya said, "The S^2 Engine's radius is shrinking... It's falling into the other side."

Late that night, the decision was made to evacuate all civilians from the Hakone caldera, beginning shortly after sunrise when the temperature had risen.

The UN offered their transports to take Eva-01 to a less-populated area, but Nerv Japan turned them down since there was no telling when the Eva might suddenly go berserk and explode. Launching it into space wasn't an option, either. The HQ facility didn't have a propulsion unit like the one used to launch the Series-0.0 Evas. Even if they did, without a way to manifest the Eva's A.T. Field, a launch wouldn't be possible. They had no means to dump Eva-01 in a remote location.

One way or another, the crisis would end in Hakone.

A torrent of evacuees clogged every road. The residents of Tokyo-3 had been told this was a temporary exodus in order to facilitate critical repairs to the city's substructure.

Such repairs had indeed been underway, but those efforts were abandoned. Once the last of the civilians had been evacuated, all work crews and Nerv personnel were ordered to flee the caldera.

The Japanese government stationed SSDF units along every highway and rail line that led from the UN-leased territory to the Japanese territory outside it. Under the guise of offering security for the evacuees, they tasked a large detachment with running inspections of the Tokyo-3 citizens at each checkpoint before transporting them away.

Aoba Shigeru had hidden himself among a line of civilians waiting for an evacuation bus. He'd concealed his identity with artificial skin and fake contact lenses, and he was armed with the best ID the intelligence division could forge. If anything could cast suspicion upon him, it was his fashion, which dated back to the previous century. The soldier at the checkpoint gave him a funny look, but the light over the gate turned green all the same, and he was waved through. Policy was policy.

The computer technician was leaving to seek assistance from a former professor, with nothing but his guitar case on his back.

Traveling by UN helicopter would have been far less hassle, but the Japanese government was vigilant against leaking valuable knowledge or personnel—especially when Nerv was the recipient. Better to travel under an identity that wouldn't draw unwanted attention.

We've always taken what we want, Aoba thought, *so, on a personal level, I sympathize with them.*

But he had no intention of returning empty-handed.

Though the S^2 Engine's functionality remained shrouded in mystery, there had been a time when scientists thought they could replicate one using human technology, with materials—like Fullerne-C60—capable of withstanding local tidal forces. A human-made S^2 Engine would have revolutionized energy.

But their understanding of the engines soon changed.

What existed of the S^2 Engines in the observable universe was only half of their whole.

This theory was first proposed by a theoretical physicist. At first, the rest of her team was unconvinced—it sounded more like science fiction than science fact—but once the data began pointing to the existence of "the other side," they realized her theory explained the engines' behavior.

Still, what exactly did that mean?

Scans of the S^2 Engine revealed two helixes entwined into a nearly perfect spherical mass. In three-dimensional space, this structure looked messy and inelegant, but when represented mathematically in two-dimensional space modeled on brane cosmology, the shape looked like a wadded-up cloth opening out, with eight antenna-like structures radiating into the braneworld.

Brane cosmology could be illustrated like this: Suppose the universe existed only in two dimensions, but gravity was not constrained by those dimensions and could instead move into a third. In other words, gravity could escape the universe. If gravitational energy could travel in any direction, then the vast majority of it would not remain on the two-dimensional plane. It would leak out of the universe.

The S^2 Engines captured that escaped energy and harnessed it.

In those higher dimensions—colloquially referred to as "the other side"—the eight antennae were theorized to extend far beyond the engine itself, with an expansive, octagonal membrane stretched across them, not unlike a parasol.

Now, the S^2 Engine was losing mass and slipping into the other side.

"This has never happened before." This was not the kind of thing Maya liked to say when her lab was a run-down Evangelion cage.

As the S^2 Engine sank deeper into the other side, the mechanism could begin retrieving energy on a colossal scale.

But now we need to put that fire out.

According to her calculations, the S^2 Engine's position in three-dimensional space would become more and more unstable. Even as she was contemplating this, the bottled-up energy began to waver.

Maya sighed. "Why does the math only work out when you don't want it to?"

One of the other scientists laughed bitterly.

It was time to make a decision. Should they escape with their lives? Or should they sacrifice themselves—not so much to duty as to the desire to see dimensions beyond their own, if only for a fleeting moment?

Both choices were hard to reject.

Maya brought the scientists back to reality.

"We're going to switch out Unit One's restraint armor. I'll get the authorization straight away, but don't wait. Start dismantling it."

Eva-01's heat had begun warming the LCL. Steam rose where the liquid met the cold outside air. Condensation formed falling droplets on the surfaces of the old cage. Eva-01 had been waiting for this moment.

Asuka had been ordered to assist with the larger-scale cleanup efforts, such as collapsed buildings and bridges. Day in and day out, as she operated Eva-02 in the urban district, Asuka let her brain subconsciously choose which of the jumbled wireless communications to decode just to distract herself. She filled her senses with as much information as she could to keep unwanted thoughts at bay.

As her giant surveyed the area around her, her eyes landed on a single point.

She noticed something no one else had, and Eva-02 automatically changed direction, stepping over the yellow tape that marked the boundary of the active work area.

When the bowl of ice had shattered, massive blocks of it had scattered all across the headquarters. One such block had struck and overturned a section of the ground armor plating, which now threatened to crush Kaji's—or rather, Shinji's—watermelon patch.

"He kept the world from ending. He relocated the garden. And in three years it's still over? That's it?"

Asuka's pent-up emotions transmitted to Eva-02, which flipped over the armor plating and—

—revealed sparse patches of green.

"Oh..."

It made for an odd sight: the red giant kneeling and scrutinizing the ground.

This small slice of the world, which Shinji had allowed to survive, was still alive.

Sediment had smothered the watermelon patch, but it had also insulated the vegetation from the arctic temperatures. Eva-02 held out its hand to the patch as if trying to feel its warmth.

Ding!

The chime from Asuka's work schedule brought her back to reality.

Shinji will come back, she told herself. *His world isn't destroyed. Maybe I can look after it until he returns.*

She prayed that this was only temporary and told herself it wouldn't be like this forever.

Several days had passed since Ayanami Quatre's rebellion and escape, and the mass-production Eva's raid.

Nearly all the snow in the city had melted, but a tremendous amount of ice remained in the lake, from which the cold air continued to seep into the city.

Asuka used her Eva's hands to gather bits of debris into a makeshift windbreak.

"I'll be back soon," Asuka said to the watermelon patch.

Eva-02 stood, dirt falling from the giant's knee shields. Asuka turned and began walking back to the city, where her work awaited.

CHAPTER 8

I N HIS OFFICE on the university campus, an associate professor in his late fifties called out to the young man he'd caught typing at his computer.

"You there! Just what do you think you're—"

"Mizusato-sensei. It's been a while," Aoba said, scratching his jaw, which still tingled from removing the artificial skin.

Mizusato grunted in annoyed surprise. "Aoba. What brings you—hey! Get your hands off of my keyboard."

"That's some welcome for a former student who's come to visit you after four years. Then again, I'm not exactly thrilled to be here myself." Aoba continued typing as he looked over his shoulder. "If you'd kept your old password, I might not have had to make the trek."

Aoba's chair creaked as he swiveled to face the older man. "So then, down to business. Where are the copies you took of the quantum wave mirror blueprints and test data?"

"I don't know what you're talking about."

"Dr. Akagi Ritsuko asked your opinion on quantum wave collapses. At the time, I'd just started at Nerv. I only found out later."

Mizusato was silent.

"If she asked for your opinion, that means she showed you the data."

More silence.

"I wonder why she asked someone outside the organization for help. You might not realize this, but our intelligence division is quite terrifying."

Mizusato remained still for moment. Then he opened the door of a small, humming refrigerator, retrieved a can of beer from its hiding place behind a bottle of mineral water, cracked open the tab, and drank it all at once.

He slammed the empty can onto his desk. "It's because the mirror can destroy Evas."

"Oh?" That was quite the statement.

"Don't get me wrong. The mirror can't produce energy on the same scale as an S^2 Engine. But an Eva's core has minute contact with other dimensions. The mirror reflects those extra-dimensional quantum waves and keeps them from crossing into our own dimension."

"In other words, it suffocates their cores."

The professor nodded.

"Okay," Aoba said, "but even if the calculations checked out, you'd never have had the means to construct the thing. It's not just shelved, it's—"

"With some minor adjustments, a mirror could boost the core instead. That's what you want, isn't it? Well, I've already done the calculations."

"What?" Another surprise.

"When Dr. Akagi saw the design, she told me it was her mother's data. That woman is scary, Aoba."

Mizusato opened the drawer of his steel desk and reached inside. He produced an envelope containing documents and an old storage device, and tossed them to Aoba.

The younger man rose. "Thanks, Sensei. Everything is still in the old Geofront, covered in dust, but we lost all our data three years ago. I'm in a hurry, and I've got to run. See you later."

"Not if I can help it!"

Where am I
A sunlit porch
It's fall.
I've never seen fall
Warm colors fill my sight
A feeling of nostalgia
Whose memory is this?
There's so much light
I can't see clearly around me
But it doesn't feel too bright
This world is like a dream and
Lend me a hand.
Mother

I'm not surprised
This feels natural

I thought of something interesting.
She says we might be able to do it if we work together
Like folding a very large bedsheet
I'm still not sure what's going on
I don't quite follow what she means
Come.
I stand
We step down into the garden
Here, I'll hold this end.
She spreads it open
Or at least that's the mental image I try to form

Following her motions, I pinch with my fingers and spread my arms wide.

A tremendous roar, like an ocean wave crashing onto the rocks, thundered through Cage Two. Its vibrations were so strong that they could rattle bone.

The technicians cried out in surprise.

The tremor kept on coming, as if a massive waterfall had appeared right beside them.

Maya dashed up to the control booth, feeling as though the air were compressing her entire body.

"What's happening?" she demanded.

The scientist watching the scanner had turned pale, and her shouted replies disappeared into the noise.

"I can't hear you!"

As a general rule, Maya stayed at least two paces away from other people, but this was an emergency. She leaned in and asked again.

"The S^2 Engine has vanished!" the scientist replied. "Could it have gone to the other side?"

"What?! If that were true, then all of the energy would also be going to the other side, and we wouldn't be able to detect it. Let me see."

Maya peered at the display, and her expression changed.

Where the S^2 Engine had been was an unmeasurable field—just a black space on the screen.

The personnel in Cage Two were all shouting at each other, trying to understand the situation.

The cage was filled with noise—not just sound, but noise of every kind—gravitational, magnetic, and radioactive.

The noise so overwhelmed the three-dimensional scanner that the system was on the brink of crashing altogether, but that wasn't what surprised Maya the most—nor was the black, unmeasurable space. What surprised her was the soup around it. The Eva's organs had begun reasserting their boundaries with terrific speed.

Except...

"This is different from before. Unit One is developing into something new."

The giant's internal structure sprang into existence with explosive force.

Where it hadn't been removed, the Type-F restraint armor was being pushed past its limits. A section of plating flew off the Eva's arm, which was now visibly larger. The remaining armor followed suit.

The technical officer shouted. "Don't stand in front of its chest!"

"Why not?" yelled an engineer.

"Because of that!"

The technical officer pointed at the cage wall facing the Eva, where a wide patch of its surface had changed color. Smoke drifted off of it, as if Eva-01 was emitting something.

"Turn off lights four, five, eight, and nine!" The technical officer ordered.

The lights in front of the Eva went dark, and a soft, pink glow remained. The effect was more pronounced in the LCL, where splintered light radiated out from Eva-01's chest.

"All personnel, put on your protective suits!" Maya shouted.

The light now seemed to be coming not from the Eva itself but from a point in space in front of its chest, as if an invisible lens floated there, pouring out a torrent of energy.

"That's proton decay," gasped a scientist in the control booth before bursting into laughter. "Ha! A never-before-seen particle, and I get to observe a dozen of them up close. Incredible!"

"Put on your protective suit," another scolded. "Those particles are flying in from extradimensional space!"

As the crew shouted back and forth, excitement and emotions running high, the service bay door slid open. They turned in unison. A crane arm entered the cage on an overhead rail. Ten wires hung from the crane, holding an armored chest piece reworked from an abandoned design—the magic mirror that could kill an Eva.

The crane brought the mirror to a stop near Eva-01, which was still shedding its own armor.

Maya shouted as loudly as she could to be heard over the waterfall roar, waving her arms broadly within her protective suit.

"Everyone, to me!"

The scientists tapped each other on the shoulder to pass the word along, while the engineers, more used to working in noisy environments, used hand signals. They gathered in front of Maya, a sea of orange protective suits.

"Is everyone all right?" Maya asked, thinking, *When did I start worrying about others?*

Her crew's eyes were wide with fear and excitement.

I bet I have the same look on my face, too.

Everyone knew that they were present for something extraordinary.

Like everyone standing before her, Maya had been thoroughly soaked by the condensation. She wiped the droplets from her glasses and dried her forehead with a sleeve. Anyone who hadn't joined this team until after the Battle at Nerv HQ was seeing her smile for the first time.

"The situation has changed, so I'll give a brief rundown.

If anyone has doubts, please share your opinion, because we're about to install the mirror."

The chest armor had a more complex shape than the standard Eva design. It was the very antithesis of grace and elegance. There was a certain artistry inherent in mechanical design, but this armor came across as the product of a designer who'd thrown everything at the wall to see what stuck.

This Eva-killer is a lot heavier than it looks.

"Until now," Maya explained, "Unit One has operated by recovering energy escaping our observable universe into the higher dimensions."

"Like recycling," offered the technical officer, a tall woman who'd placed herself at Maya's side.

"But now that extradimensional energy is cascading over to our side completely unchecked."

"Too much of a good thing!" said the technical officer.

"Right now, Unit One's body is transforming at an incredible pace. But this is *not* some kind of self-destruct sequence. The Eva is not trying to discard its body, nor is it going to release all that energy."

The crew erupted, but Maya brought them to order.

"However, the estimated volume of this energy is increasing proportionally with the speed of Unit One's growth." Maya pointed to a chart indicating the predicted levels. "At this mark here, the reconstruction of its body should be complete. But look how the energy keeps rising after."

The line remained nearly straight all the way off the chart.

"If we can't get the energy under control," Maya continued, "the reconstruction process will run haywire until it finally breaks down. The end result will be self-destruction, and we have no way of knowing how much damage it will cause."

Maya looked at the faces of her crew. She had their complete attention.

"Start attaching the prototype restraint armor!" Maya shouted. Her throat was getting scratchy; she wasn't used to speaking so loudly. "The mirror will keep reflecting the energy back on itself until it returns to the other side—hopefully before our universe is torn apart through the extradimensional window."

For the second time in several days, an attack alarm added itself to the noise of the cage.

But the technical officer ordered the crew to keep working. "Equipment and transport teams, come with me to Cage One. Everyone else, follow Chief Ibuki's commands and start installing that armor!"

The cluster of orange bodies hustled off in two directions.

Toji appeared at the entrance to the cage. "Heya! I heard you needed as many people as you could get, so I came to help with the physical stuff!"

Maya pressed a damp protective suit into his hands and barked, "Wear this!" Then, with some surprise, she added, "Why didn't you evacuate? You have family, don't you—a sister?"

"Yeah, I was leaving 'cause of that, but before we got out of

the caldera, I decided to check in on Shinji, and then—" Toji un-
folded the soggy suit with a look of disgust but put it on anyway.
"Well, the alarm went off. Sis is in the lobby watching our bags.
Anyway, what's all this noise?"

Maya pointed at the LCL. Steam rose from its surface.

"Look, no coffin makes that much of a racket. Maya-san,
Shinji's—"

"He's still melted inside there."

CHAPTER 9

ELECTROMAGNETIC BLITZ

ALARMS SOUNDED throughout Tokyo-3. Another threat had come, same as it had ever been. Nerv was rarely the aggressor; the hostile entities mostly came to them.

Starting with Rei Quatre's rebellion, that troublesome cycle seemed to be starting again.

In a holding cell in the interrogation office, Rei Trois heard the alarm, and her shoulders twitched.

She let out a startled gasp and immediately tried to connect to the other Ayanamis.

It was a reflexive response driven into her through training. She couldn't see Quatre, but for a split second, she connected to Cinq and Six—or at least she felt like she did—but that was all. Then, once again, she was alone.

The guard stationed in Rei's cell stood and said something to her, but she only trembled.

Dressed formally, Commander Katsuragi Misato entered the command center. She had just returned from the government offices of Tokyo-2, where she had gone to explain the decision to terminate Eva-01. On the way back, her heavy VTOL aircraft stopped to pick up Aoba, who had taken off running toward Cage Two the moment they arrived.

Inside the command center, Rei Cinq and Rei Six were talking over each other, their voices coming through the room's speakers from orbit.

"What's going on? Report," Misato said.

"A single, large-scale threat is approaching from the direction of Mount Myojogatake," Hyuga replied. "We have visual conformation that it's the same type as the Angel Carrier that previously attacked us."

Angel Carrier. That was the name Misato had chosen for the animated corpse of the mass-production Eva that had carried Sachiel in its cocoon.

"That close?! Why didn't our radar or satellites see it?"

Whatever trick the Angel Carrier had employed, it had managed to slip through Nerv's long-range detection systems—both visual and seismic. By the time it had been noticed, it was mere kilometers east of HQ.

"And what's with these two talking?" Misato asked.

"They suddenly woke up and started talking to each other," Hyuga said, "not through the mental link, but over the terrestrial monitoring frequency."

"What about Trois? The mental mirroring?"

"Apparently, she was able to briefly connect with them. The two in orbit have a detectable time lag between their brain waves, so I think she's telling the truth."

"Why did they wake up?"

The clones had been speaking at such a breakneck pace that the staff inside the command center at Hakone hadn't been able to decipher any meaning. The prevailing theory was that the pair shared identical knowledge, and their conversation simply skipped over everything they didn't need to say. But before that theory could be put to the test, the clones' conversation had started to break down, approaching total incoherence.

Misato quickly grasped the danger.

"Stop them!" she shouted. "Their minds are going to break. Make them go back to sleep. Return their brain activity and metabolic control to sustainable levels."

By the time the pair had been induced back into a deep sleep, their vitals were off the charts.

As long as the pilots were not of sound mind, the S² Engine-powered Evas and their gamma-ray laser cannons had to remain out of play. The search-and-destroy system Nerv Japan had spent two years developing only functioned through a single teenage girl, and because the system relied on her, it was now effectively useless.

《Attention! The SSDF forces in Gora have begun an attack.》

The screen switched to the main tower's camera, which showed the purple-tinged eastern sky. A few seconds later, the image shook.

"We've received a communication from the commanding officer of the SSDF guard forces," Hyuga reported. "They have engaged the enemy at 1035 hours. Due to ongoing civilian evacuation, air support is being withheld."

Frustrated, Misato said, "Then they should have prioritized the evacuation and waited to engage. Guide the civilians to the nearest shelters."

At the foot of the eastern mountains, the curved neck of a beam cannon briefly came into view before firing. The beam's focal point blasted the bare surface of the mountain.

Misato squinted at the screen. "What is that?"

The dazzling beam of light converged on the Angel Carrier on the far side of the ridge. Airborne particles caught by the beam were scattered, forming a curtain of lightning bolts.

The image brought Hyuga to his feet. "Incredible."

"It's the SSDF's new maser howitzer! So *that's* what was on the pair of armored flatbeds that came in to Yumoto."

"I know we have our own maser beams for power transmission, but I never expected this."

The maser cannon couldn't put out as much energy as Nerv's gamma-ray laser or positron rifles. But the weapon could focus its beam for nearly four seconds uninterrupted, resulting in a higher cumulative energy output. The maser's tremendous energy requirements were supplied by an N_2 reactor, which had been developed alongside Jet Alone's successor.

The Angel Carrier quickly put up a field, but not before the maser beam, using a reflector at the end of the cannon's arm to

TYPE-3 PROTOTYPE MASER HOWITZER

A mobile weapon for suppressing Angel-scale threats; deployed by the Japan Strategic Self-Defense Force outside the Hakone caldera after the area was designated as UN-leased land. A miniaturized N_2 Reactor provides the substantial power required to project the microwaves from its laser.

focus on a single point, struck its target—the cocoon inside the Carrier's rib cage.

"So then," Misato said, "everything we learned in that battle..."

"It looks like they found out," Hyuga added.

The rest of the beam's energy was deflected by the Carrier's shield and scorched the mountainside.

"And yet they withdrew Akashima to Tokyo-2, claiming they didn't want to be involved in the destruction of Unit One."

"I hadn't heard anything about them completing the maser cannon," Hyuga said. "Do you think they're using this as a field test where they don't have to worry about repercussions? If the maser doesn't work, it's still our mess to clean up."

The Angel Carrier rocked backward—

"It's not stopping," Misato said. "Send out the surveillance drone."

—and squatted down.

Wait.

For a moment, the Angel Carrier appeared to have been immobilized, but it was simply gathering strength in its legs. In the next moment, it leaped high into the air. The giant turned, mid-flight. When it landed, it was a considerable distance away, the SSDF maser howitzer crushed under its feet.

"Incredible!" Hyuga said. "Did the maser miss the mark, or was it simply not strong enough to punch through?"

"One of those," Misato said. "Is it just me, or does this Carrier look a little different from the first one? Its shoulders are more like our Evas."

Indeed, some kind of plating appeared to be sticking out on either side of the Carrier's head.

Eva-02's icon began blinking on the status board, accompanied by a pleasant electronic chime.

《I'm bringing up Unit Two with the rectenna.》Asuka said. 《I'm counting on you to have the maser transmitters ready. I'd been hoping to borrow power from the SSDF, but they didn't last very long, did they?》

"I wouldn't advise putting yourself on the receiving end of that cannon," Hyuga said, responding to Asuka's joke in earnest. "A maser beam that focused wouldn't give you power, it would punch a hole right through your rectenna!"

"Are our maser transmission towers ready?" Misato asked.

"Raised and calibrated."

"Asuka, I love your confidence, but don't forget that you're our last defense."

The only Eva that Nerv Japan could currently field was Asuka's.

The orbital sniper network—Nerv's supposed ace in the hole—could no longer be counted on. They still had Eva-00, but its pilot was Rei Trois, and there were fears she might end up going the same route as Quatre.

And Unit-01 was...

Asuka shook the thoughts from her head. "Unit Two launching!"

Her right hand held the Lance of Longinus.

When Eva-02 emerged from the eastern gate, it wasn't trailing an umbilical cable.

A folded frame on its left shoulder pylon opened in the shape of a large cross.

"Rectenna open."

《Beginning transmission in five seconds... Two, one, mar—》

Kzzk!

Interference cut off Hyuga's countdown, but Asuka didn't panic.

"Receiving maser beam. Power gain is within tolerances."

《Unit Two, this is the command center.》 Hyuga had switched to a different communication band. 《Direct the battle away from the monorail station. We have civilians there.》

"Acknowledged, command center. If I get anywhere near that area, cut my power. I don't want to vaporize the evacuees."

Maser transmission towers stood all around Tokyo-3, aside from a few areas where line of sight was restricted, such as the ravines between the mountains and some lakeside sections. This infrastructure had been forced on Nerv Japan by the UN, under whose auspices Nerv Japan existed. It was the global community's way of protesting Nerv's decision to equip the Series-0.0 Evas with S^2 Engines. Their message was clear: stick with cables and beams.

This power transmission was efficient enough to free an Eva from its umbilical cable, but the electromagnetic interference reduced its efficacy by more than half. Still, the maser method was useful in cases such as this, where the Eva needed to go beyond the cable's reach.

The transmission towers swiveled in unison to follow Eva-02's movements. Powered by ultra-short coherent waves, the Eva walked up the slopes with the rectenna upon its shoulder, like a massive cross.

The spillover microwaves turned to heat and light, crackling across the surface of Asuka's A.T. Field.

In the chaos of Cage Two, the attachment of Eva-01's new chest piece had hit a snag. While the mirror was being moved into place, the overhead crane brought in a separate piece of armor—a headpiece with boxy, angular facets and a curved, bow-like horn. Siren lights spun to warn the crew that the crane was in motion. An alarm blared as well, though the sound couldn't be heard over the Eva's thunderous rumble.

"You're even replacing the headpiece?" Toji asked Maya.

"What? I can't hear you!"

Toji patted his safety helmet and tried again. "Are. You. Replacing. The. Headpiece?"

"Yes!" Maya shouted. "This restraint armor is bigger all around. Whoever designed it must have anticipated the Eva having a truly beastly body. You can feel the designer's fear in the work. See how there's an armored visor that can be lowered to cover its eyes?"

"I don't know. Feels macabre."

The crane stopped, and the headpiece swayed.

"A little more to the right!"

The crane's range fell just short of Eva-01. The engineers began pulling at a rope hanging from the headpiece, and the scientists joined them.

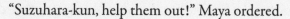

"Suzuhara-kun, help them out!" Maya ordered.

"Going analog, are we?"

"We're not working on a factory line. This is what one-off builds are like."

Toji would have a chance to learn that for himself if he took a job at a workshop. He was at that time in high school when teachers started asking their students about future plans. Of course, the students were talking among themselves, too. But as Toji pulled the rope, somehow the future no longer felt real—not just his future, but the world's.

Asuka considered the situation. The eastern evacuation route and the monorail lay between her and the Angel Carrier. *In that case...*

"Command, I'm going to circle around to the north. You saw how the Angel Carrier destroyed the maser. This one is actively on the attack."

The previous mass-production Eva's only goal had been to reach the Chronostatic Sphere, and it had ignored anything not directly in its path.

《You think you can draw it away?》Misato asked.

"*Ja,* boss. I'm closing the rectenna. Cease power transmission."

Eva-02 sprinted across the foothills of Mount Daigatake and crossed Highway 138 to the north of Mount Kozuka. When Asuka had positioned herself northwest of the Angel Carrier, she unfurled the rectenna again.

She slammed the butt of the Lance of Longinus into the ground and shifted the Powered 8—the next-gen pallet rifle—from a one-handed to a two-handed grip.

"Switching to burst-fire mode."

The entry plug's AI chimed and tightened the aiming reticle for accuracy.

"I'm not really looking for accuracy, but sure," Asuka said. "Command center, Unit Two initiating fire."

Three shots cracked through the air.

Unlike an A.T. Field, the Carrier's power shield was invisible. But when Eva-02's three bullets struck the shield's surface, the tremendous kinetic energy produced rainbow-colored pillars of flame.

"Hey, you! Look over here!" Asuka shouted.

As if it could hear her from three kilometers away, the Angel Carrier turned—and held out its hand.

"Huh?"

The air distorted. Asuka dropped her left hand from the Powered 8's foregrip. No sooner had she grasped the Lance of Longinus than—

Wham!

She felt like she'd been struck by an ocean wave, and Eva-02 was knocked back with tremendous force.

Startled voices erupted throughout the command center, where Eva-02 appeared on the main screen.

"What the hell just happened?!" Misato asked.

Asuka replied as if the answer were obvious. 《That thing threw its power shield at me. The question is, did it come up with that trick on its own, or did it see me and Shinji do the same thing?》

"Are you suggesting it was around back then?"

《I don't know. I wanted to hear how it sounded.》

The roar inside Cage Two startled Aoba, but he hurried across the catwalk and into the old, dusty control booth. Maya began inputting the professor's hard-copy data while Aoba fed the Magi system what was on the storage device.

Toji didn't understand what they were doing. "So, what, you put that mirror thing around him, and everything's just fine?"

"Say you had a normal mirror," Maya replied, "and you wanted to use it to reflect light at a particular spot. That would require some careful, precise adjustments, right?"

"Yeah, I guess."

"This restraint armor was originally designed by Dr. Akagi to permanently freeze an Eva's core."

"And that will keep the Eva from self-destructing?"

"Unfortunately," Aoba interjected, "it's not that simple anymore now that Eva-01's all worked up. Even if we cut it off from the dimensions on the other side, there's so much energy flowing through that it would break the mirror and keep coming. Frankly, I'm stunned by what I'm seeing."

"That's why we're changing plans," Maya said, still pounding the keys. "But like I said, it's going to take careful, precise adjustments. We're going to redirect the stream of energy and prevent it from expanding the extradimensional window any further. If we get to that point, and everything goes well, then we can think about what comes next."

Above ground, a long-range battle of rifle versus invisible shields had begun.

As Asuka had planned, the Angel Carrier changed course and began closing in on Eva-02. But her enemy hadn't moved as far away from the city and its transportation network as she wanted. Continuing her patient retreat to the northern wall of the caldera, she evaded the Carrier's shield attacks, occasionally firing back to keep her opponent's attention.

And then—

"This is far enough."

She went on the attack. Eva-02 folded its rectenna again, stowed the Powered 8 on its rail mount, and took the Lance of Longinus in hand. Asuka sped toward the Angel Carrier, dodging left and right around the incoming shields.

"Just as I thought! When I change directions, there's a short delay before it reacts. Which means..."

Accelerating to top speed, she projected her A.T. Field in a cone ahead of her and dove headfirst into the Angel Carrier.

The field shot across the ground, shredding the surface and kicking up great clouds of dust, yet still preserving all its tremendous kinetic energy for when it slammed into the Angel Carrier's shield. With a deafening roar, the two barriers met, light cascading like fireworks from their plane of contact. But the Carrier's shield held, deflecting Eva-02's charge.

The Carrier turned sideways to pursue the cone of Eva-02's A.T. Field, and Asuka saw her opening.

The tips of the Lance of Longinus appeared from the dust cloud. Eva-02 hadn't passed the Angel Carrier, it had projected the A.T. Field forward while remaining behind.

Separated from its field, Eva-02 thrust the lance, and its two red prongs pierced the Carrier's red, glowing cocoon all the way through.

Cheers erupted in the command center.

Asuka had struck the Carrier's weakest point before the larval Angel inside it even had a chance to come out.

"That was great, Asuka!" Misato said. "But isn't that cheating?"

《Shut up,》 Asuka replied, playing along, but—

Something doesn't feel right. I should've met more resistance.

"What?!"

Asuka reacted with confusion and then surprise.

A powerful force was pulling the lance, past the point where there should have been anywhere for it to go, deep enough that the weapon's twin tips should have already emerged from the Angel Carrier's back.

The Carrier's power shield slammed into Eva-02's arms and forced it to release the lance.

The shield's impact shredded the cocoon, revealing a black-and-white-patterned sphere consuming the lance.

"Leliel!" Misato sprang to her feet.

The Angel Leliel.

The black-and-white moiré sphere was only the Angel's shadow. The Angel itself inhabited a pocket of imaginary space within the sphere and could swallow up anything and everything.

"We've been tricked!"

The Angel Carrier came here to steal our copy of the lance.

But what good was knowing the enemy's plan when it had already been achieved?

Once the Lance of Longinus had been swallowed whole, Leliel's shadow vanished from the cocoon.

Asuka was furious.

Eva-02 detached the microwave rectenna from its shoulder, plunged the giant cross into the ground at the Angel Carrier's feet, and jumped away.

《Hyuga, burn it!》

In the command center, Hyuga scrambled for the controls.

Two nearby towers, and three distant ones with trajectories only narrowly passing above the terrain, blasted their maser beams at the rectenna in unison.

Without external management, the five microwave beams rapidly overcharged the rectenna. In an instant, its capacitors' superconductive lattice broke down.

Eva-02's vision filled with white.

Multiple terawatts powered the resulting electromagnetic explosion. The steel frames of the nearby transmission towers melted from the induced current, and their concrete foundations disintegrated like sand. The water in the soil surrounding evaporated, and the ground in a five-hundred-meter radius swelled and then exploded.

Asuka retrieved the Powered 8 from her shoulder rail.

The timer for her internal battery reserves raced toward zero. Beyond her HUD rose a mushroom cloud streaked with lightning, and from it, the Angel Carrier emerged.

"Yeah," Asuka said, "you *would* survive that, wouldn't you? You know, I think I'm starting to dislike you."

Asuka heard a sound.

Thud!

At first, she thought it was her own heart racing.

Thwump! Thwump! Thwump!

But it seemed...distant. *Where is that coming from?*

Her eyes were locked on the Angel Carrier, but for some reason, she was transfixed by the sound.

"What is it?"

NEON GENESIS
EVANGELION ANIMA

CHAPTER 10

TRANSFERENCE

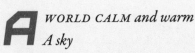 WORLD CALM and warm
A sky
The object my mother and I unfolded sways in the breeze
We sit on the edge of the porch
Watching

If everything is coming to an end—
Says the person I perceive to be my mother
—we'll need to fold that back up and take it inside before twilight.
Why?
This power is too great.
But just as it took two to unfold it, it can't be folded alone.
You need to find someone to help you.
But I have you
Can't we fold it together?
I have to leave my existence here.
The white world turns even brighter

The image of my mother fades into the light
Goodbye.
Mother, what are you going to do?
There's somewhere I want to go.
And then...
In this moment
I realize her presence has been with me all along
Without form
But many times my savior
And now she's leaving
Shinji, I leave everything in your hands.
My thoughts are hazy as I begin to cry
Pitifully
Shamelessly
I cry

The roar in Cage Two had changed.
Hm? Toji thought. *Is the sound starting to vacillate?*
The all-encompassing rumble ebbed and flowed like waves against a shore.

Aoba noticed Toji's expression and said, "The wavelengths are converging." He looked down from the command deck. "We're almost there! East side, adjust by .01."

The eastern group pulled their rope in unison.

The ever-present, pulsing rumble scattered little parts from the chest plate, which despite being the first piece of armor the crew had attempted to install, was now the only piece still out of place. The rest of the restraint armor had been attached amid the tumult.

"West side, adjust by .002 to .03—slowly now!"

Toji had joined the line of workers on the west, and he added the strength of his artificial arms.

The pounding, waterfall-like noise changed tenor and began to oscillate between quiet and loud. But with each cycle, it grew quieter, until it had faded nearly to nothing.

In unison, the teams took a deep breath, then—

Thud!

The sudden sound, loud but singular, elicited startled cries around the room.

Pinned down within the quantum wave mirror, Eva-01's chest vibrated as if something were bouncing around inside it.

Aoba snapped his fingers. "That's the spot! We've got it perfectly centered. Secure the mirror! Mathematically, this is as close as we can get. The interference wave is less than five trillionths of the amplitude."

Thud!

The sound shook the room. Everyone turned and look up.

"He's born. I'm glad he came back."

"What did you say?" Maya asked Toji, who'd almost sounded like he'd been making a prophecy.

"Hm? Did I say something?" Toji appeared to snap out of a trance.

Maya scanned the Eva's internals, but after being battered by soundwaves, the scanning array's resolution had been reduced by more than half, and the resulting image wasn't clear.

"But he's still..."

Thud!

Maya jolted in surprise as everything around her rattled and shook.

The scanner array produced a picture of the Eva's interior in disjointed fragments.

Its internal structure was re-forming. The divisions were beginning to stabilize.

Thud!

New boundaries were being set—here the skeleton, there the muscle.

When Shinji had first piloted Eva-01 into battle, its eye had regenerated when Shinji looked at the reflection of its exposed body in the windows of a tall building. Now the Eva's entire body was like that—not a mere imitation of the human form, but a reflection of humanity itself.

Evas weren't organic in nature, and no blood flowed through them. But when they were cut, they sprayed blood, and they even decomposed like organic matter. Due to quantum teleportation, every part of their massive, hundred-meter-tall bodies was connected—as if they had a nervous system—and the giants could respond with the same agility as humans.

Thud!

"This seems less like an interference wave and more like…"

Evas didn't have hearts, but the remains of Eva-01's S^2 Engine pulsed like a heartbeat.

The torrential river of energy, now tamed, that had brought rebirth—and very nearly destruction—beat within the Eva's chest.

Thud!

The sound was still plenty terrifying.

Outside, Eva-02 was struggling against an Angel Carrier's assault. A great number of civilians had likely been caught in the battle, not to mention SSDF soldiers.

And yet, the personnel in Cage Two were excited and smiling—some even laughed. There was no logic to their behavior; it just was.

Thud!

The rhythm was primal; the rhythm of new life.

Thud!

The sound was like fireworks launching close by. Swept up in the excitement, Toji howled, "Listen to it go!"

Thud!

An engineer started drumming the handrail with a spanner in time with the beat. Soon, everyone had joined in—not just the engineers but the scientists, too. Everyone found something to make noise with.

Fwump! Fwump! Fwump!

This was the sound Asuka had heard.

In the command center, Misato heard it, too.

"What is that?"

The commander was in a separate building, one that had been hardened against explosions and earthquakes. The sound shouldn't have carried into that space, and yet there it was, both distant and close.

Thwump! Thwump! Thwump!

As the engineers and scientists reveled, new organs came to life within Eva-01—larger bones, stronger muscles, and, finally, a small human figure.

Rei Trois lifted her head.

"The scent is changing... Someone is crying... Is it...Ikari-kun?"

CHAPTER 11

ONTO THE STAGE

ASUKA STARED DOWN the sights of her Powered 8 at the Angel Carrier. The white giant was coming toward her, and then it suddenly stopped.

The Carrier looked toward the source of the sound that wasn't a sound.

Thud!

In Cage Two, Eva-01 sensed it was being watched and raised its head, visor still closed—as if it could see through metal, stone, and earth—to look back at its observer.

"It's moving!" Aoba said.

There was another loud noise, this time from the locks on the gantry supports as the steel latches snapped apart. The Eva easily tore free from the external restraint devices, which had been weakened, but not broken, up to this point.

As multi-ton objects flew through the air like pebbles, smashing into the heat-blasted concrete wall, the crew finally came back to their senses.

The rumbling of destruction filled the room.

"Everyone, evacuate the cage!" someone shouted, and the teams started running.

Suddenly self-conscious of her part in their irrational revelry, Maya blushed. "What...were we doing?"

"We can talk about that later!" Aoba shouted, pulling her arm.

Toji looked over his shoulder. "Shinji? Are you doing this?"

"Later," Aoba repeated. "Let's get out of here!"

Misato tried to connect to Cage One.

"Maya! Chief Ibuki, is this commotion coming from your building? Are you there?"

Someone cried out from the middle deck, and Misato's eyes darted to the main screen, which displayed an image from one of the exterior cameras. *That's over at the far edge of the HQ.*

The dome of Cage Two blasted into the sky.

A purple giant burst out into the world, as if nothing in heaven or on earth could stand in its way.

"Is that..." Misato squinted in disbelief. "Unit One?"

Still smoldering from Asuka's full-power EM attack, the Angel Carrier paid no heed to Eva-02 and began walking in the direction of the sound that wasn't a sound.

"Hey!"

Asuka prepared to launch another attack that she knew would be futile. Eva-02's hand dropped as the giant crouched to charge, when suddenly the ground began to vibrate, fast and strong, with no discernible source.

Where is that coming from? Asuka asked herself. And then she knew the answer—the other side of Mount Kozuka.

In the next instant, a figure came leaping over the mountaintop. The figure was huge, growing larger as it drew closer. And then it landed, cratering the earth and sending chunks of dirt and stone flying.

"Unit One? Is that you? Shinji?"

Eva-01 didn't respond. The purple giant wore armor Asuka hadn't seen before, moving nimbly despite its rugged appearance.

Without pause, Eva-01 went on the attack, slamming into the Angel Carrier's shield. The two giants stared each other down.

Asuka let out a startled yelp. "Shinji! This bastard's shield is strong. Put up your A.T. Field before you get killed!"

But Eva-01 ignored her and repeated its charge.

Has it gone berserk?

The Eva pounded its fists against the Carrier's shield to no effect—or at least, that's what Asuka thought until its arm suddenly penetrated the shield amid a shower of sparks and grabbed the Carrier's face.

"What?" Asuka blurted. *What's happening?*

Before she could recover from her shock, Eva-01 had crushed the Carrier's face. The Eva's hand and arm plates glowed, bands of interference dancing across the surface of its body.

"What?" Asuka repeated. "The Eva isn't projecting an A.T. Field outside itself. It's generating one along the contours of its body!"

Nobody can do that—and even if they could, it would immobilize them. How is Unit One moving?!

Not about to be discouraged by a crushed face, the Angel Carrier swung its staff, but Eva-01 dodged the attack and sprang into the air with such extraordinary force that the ground beneath its feet erupted like a giant column of water.

Is this thing still an Eva?

Eva-01 landed on the Carrier's shield from above. The shield withstood the impact but was thrown to the ground along with its wielder. They bounced once before coming to a stop. The ground liquified from the impact, and when Eva-01 stomped on the shield again, the force of the blow buried the Carrier more than halfway.

"Unit One is out of control," Asuka said.

Misato, in the command center, must have sensed the same danger. 《Asuka, put some distance between yourself and Unit One. The Eva isn't responding to us. There's a chance it won't be able to distinguish friend from foe.》

Is there, though?

In that pulsing beat, Asuka had felt her own heart yearning to join in. It was a feeling of something shared... Emotion, maybe.

Together, they had kept the same rhythm.

The Angel Carrier cleared away the sediment with its shield and lurched to its feet.

This Carrier, unlike the previous one, had two shoulder pylons resembling those of an Evangelion. On the fronts of the pylons were black sigils, and Asuka let out a breath as she saw them turn red and begin to glow.

Those pylons...

Asuka had seen those sigils and their red glow before—in the Geofront, on the first Angel Carrier she'd defeated, in the empty cocoon that had held Sachiel.

And this one has two? On its shoulders?!

Eva-02 stood up straight. Asuka knew what she needed to do. She would wait for Eva-01 to leap at the Carrier again. Then she'd come from the monster's left, since the staff was in its right hand.

She circled around to the opposite side. Every moment mattered. Her internal battery was nearly drained.

The moment she was waiting for came quickly. Eva-01 pounced on the Angel Carrier, and the Carrier summoned its shield around its staff, swinging from left to right.

Just as I thought—the Carrier is focused entirely on Unit One.

"A lucky win is still a win!"

Asuka aimed the Powered 8 at the plate on the Carrier's exposed shoulder and emptied the pallet gun.

The rifle had been down to six bullets, and the railgun mechanism fired all of them so quickly that they made one continuous report. The shoulder plate shattered into red, crystalline fragments.

Eva-01 dropped to all fours and ducked under the staff.

The Carrier continued its sweeping motion and threw the staff at Eva-02, hitting it in the stomach and sending Asuka reeling.

Through bleary eyes, she saw Eva-01 deliver a crouching kick to the Angel Carrier. *It's so incredibly strong.*

Eva-01 had broken the Carrier's leg in a single strike.

Fighting through the intense feedback pain, Asuka shouted as loudly as she could manage. "Shinji! Finish it!"

Shinji could see. He jumped to his feet.

Eva-01's visor lifted, and its eyes opened.

The world was beautiful. The world was ugly.

Shinji's mind raced to process the sudden abundance of information that filled his view. But before he could even comprehend the state of the battle, his body moved by instinct.

The Angel Carrier had one shoulder pylon remaining.

《The plate!》 Shinji shouted, and everyone connected over Nerv Japan's communication link heard him.

The heavily armored giant spun with surprising speed and kicked out with its right leg. A cloud trailed from the tip of its foot. When the kick connected, the overwhelming force shattered the Angel Carrier's shield and the remaining shoulder plate.

Red, crystalline shards scattered like a spray of blood, only to vanish before they even hit the ground. The Angel Carrier collapsed like a marionette whose strings had snapped. It flopped onto the dirt, a corpse again.

The mass-production Eva quickly disintegrated.

Eva-01 looked around. Eva-02 was kneeling, its internal battery fully spent. Somehow, Asuka's Eva seemed smaller than it had before.

"Asuka... What's going on?"

《I'd like to ask you the same thing.》

Nerv

GOD'S IN HIS HEAVEN ALL'S RIGHT WITH THE WORLD

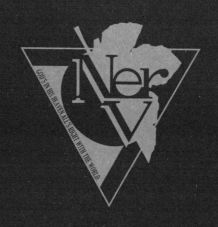

PART 3

NEON GENESIS

A PLANET STRANGLED

EVANGELION: ANIMA

NEON GENESIS
EVANGELiON ANIMA

CHAPTER 12

HOMECOMING

T HE NEAR-COLLISION ALARM sounded in Eva-01's entry plug, followed by Asuka's voice.

《Wait! Code Unit One!》

Eva-02 charged recklessly to catch up to Eva-01.

The wind howled, and the streetlights shook.

《Command center to Unit Two. Don't run.》 Hyuga's voice was urgent. 《Follow protocol when re-entering the base. We have to pay for anything you step on or destroy outside of combat!》

Asuka didn't care about that. While fighting the Angel Carrier, she'd called Shinji's name. Now she wanted to make sure he was really in there.

《Shinji! Is that you, Shinji?》

Asuka opened a two-way video transmission. She appeared on Shinji's HUD, and he appeared on hers. When she saw him, her mouth dropped, but Shinji couldn't read her expression.

She frowned, glaring at him. 《Say something.》

Shinji was confused. *What's gotten into her?*

"Asuka, watch behind you. I'll keep watch this way!"

By standing in front of him, Eva-02 was blocking the area where his visual sensors were strongest. He turned away, not to ignore her, but because he was still wary of other attackers.

Shinji didn't fully understand the situation. To him, the battle was still raging.

He focused on his Eva's senses, but between the residual heat from the fight with the Angel Carrier and the search-and-rescue teams clogging the skies and roads, he couldn't get a clear read on any potential enemy emissions.

In frustration, he said, "Hyuga-san, are you sure there aren't any more enemies? What about Quatre's Eva-0.0?"

《Shinji?》 Asuka sounded perplexed.

Hyuga let the questions hang in the air for a moment before responding.

《This is Hakone command to...Code Unit One.》

That was an odd way of phrasing his call sign. *Wait... Asuka called me that, too.*

Hyuga continued. 《Unit Quatre disappeared following the battle on the lake. There's been no trace of her since.》

She might be setting us up for an ambush. I need to be on alert for a long-range attack, but why is Hyuga acting like the battle happened a while ago?

Misato jumped on the comm channel.

《Shinji-kun.》 A stilted pause. 《If your external connections have been restored...look at your calendar.》

My calendar? What is she—

Shinji gasped.

More than a few days had passed since Shinji's last memory.

He immediately doubted what he was seeing. The AI picked up on his misgivings and reset the clock three times, even trying different sources and displaying each in turn. *Tactical link. Radio signal. GPS satellite.*

But the time and date remained the same.

"What's going on?" Shinji asked. "What happened?"

《I'll explain in person.》 Misato said. 《For now, I just want to say... I'm glad you came back, Shinji-kun.》

She's talking like I've been on a long trip. Something is really strange here.

《Proceed to the underground transport to Cage Two. And...》

Shinji's mind spun, the commander's voice fading into the distance, when—

Beep! Beep! Beep!

The near-collision alarm sounded again, and then—*Beeeeep!*—impact.

Eva-02 slammed into his back.

Shinji yelped, and his reborn Eva-01—which would soon receive the name Super Evangelion—staggered forward.

Asuka finished Misato's sentence.

《Welcome home, Shinji.》

I think I was dreaming about my mother.

And my Eva is really hot. I don't know what's happened to it.

The environmental controls inside the cockpit read normal. But this oppressive heat...

Thump!

"What's that sound?"

The Eva's chest reverberated repeatedly just on the other side of his entry plug display. Every time it did, Shinji felt as if something hot was pumping through the Eva's body—and his own.

Thump!

"Command, I think Unit One is broken."

《Yeah, well, I can't say you're wrong about that.》 On the screen, Misato laughed. It was a bitter laugh...but a laugh all the same. 《That's your body—that's your Eva. Super Evangelion.》

"Can we talk about the name? Oh, and by the way... Why am I naked?"

CHAPTER 13

HEARTBEAT

SHINJI PUT ON the jumpsuit someone had kindly tossed into the plug. When he emerged, he was startled by the crowd packed onto Cage Two's deck and scaffolds.

"Why are there so many people here?" he asked.

The crew had brought Eva-01's S^2 Engine back from the brink of slipping into the other side. They'd returned to the cage, which now had a massive hole in the roof from Super Eva's awakening, to see Shinji.

More had gathered than just the cage's crew. No one had believed that a living human being could be reconstituted inside an Eva, and the news had spread quickly. Naturally, people were curious to see.

Wondering what kind of miracle had taken place, personnel from all over the HQ had pressed their way into the cage. They drummed along with the Eva's heartbeat, some slapping hands on railings, others stomping their feet on the deck. The excitement and noise were that of a festival.

But when Shinji set foot on the deck, the first accident happened immediately.

Purely out of habit, Shinji raised his arm to remove his interface headset, which he wasn't even wearing.

The crowd cheered in delight and surprise. Shinji turned to look over his shoulder and gasped.

Behind him, the familiar-but-alien Eva-01 had raised its arm, mimicking Shinji's motion, and crumpled one of the cage's side restraint units.

"Super Eva!" Shinji said with astonishment.

Metal shrieked as the steel frame of the restraint unit splintered.

A large shard hit the deck next to Shinji and bounced away.

Shinji was still synchronized with the Eva even though he had left the entry plug.

The cheers turned to panicked screams.

Shinji shrunk into himself, clutching his hand to his chest, and then he noticed another abnormality.

"He's got no heart," Toji said to Rei Trois.

After he had taken his sister home, he went straight back to Nerv HQ. Sure, he had already helped bring Shinji back to life, but not everything had wrapped up smoothly, and he wanted to stay involved.

Because Maya had her hands full recalibrating Super Eva, Toji went in her stead to check on Ayanami Trois.

Rei Trois was still under suspicion of causing Quatre to go berserk.

The interrogations by both the intelligence and security teams had produced few answers, and she was currently being held under twenty-four-hour surveillance inside a laboratory control room under the purview of the science department.

Trois had said that she didn't know Quatre's location and that, except for the one brief connection, her mental mirror link with the other Ayanamis remained broken, at least as far as she could tell. She was seated on a metal folding chair, and her expression remained as inscrutable as ever. Toji couldn't tell if she was in pain or if she was fine.

As he regarded her stoic expression, Toji thought, *She might at least try blinking.*

As if on cue, her long lashes moved, her eyelids briefly covering her ruby red eyes.

"He doesn't have a heart," she said, "but he's still alive?"

"Yep. And his blood is still pumping." Toji mimicked the thump of a beating heart.

"Thump," Ayanami Trois' lips barely moved as she repeated the word, almost as if she was chewing on it.

"And get this, Super Eva has a heart now, or something like one. The S² Engine went through a transformation."

"Super Eva?"

"Yeah. Super Eva."

In the cafeteria, Asuka blocked Maya's path. "What do you mean when you say that Shinji and his Eva are one?"

"I mean exactly that. Physically speaking, that's what's happening." Maya put the sandwich on her tray into a paper bag. Apparently finished with this conversation, she turned to leave.

"Hey!" Asuka protested. "Wait just a minute!"

Asuka shoved her tray, lunch and all, into the hands of a nearby worker.

Asuka strode briskly after Maya, her eyes level with the whorl in the woman's hair. She wondered when she had grown taller than Maya.

Still, the woman was walking faster than Asuka had expected. She was having difficulty keeping up.

Her mind tried to make sense of what Maya had said. *The Eva is the Eva, and Shinji is Shinji. They* aren't *one. Maybe she means...*

"Was Shinji birthed from the Eva?"

"That might be part of it," Maya answered without stopping.

"Do Shinji and the Eva share a heart?"

"Maybe."

Oh, come on!

Asuka decided to say something, even if she wasn't quite ready to hear it herself. She steeled herself.

"All right, so that mama's boy had a dream where his...mother... disappeared."

What did this mean for the origin and future of her own Eva?

Sometimes when she was in Unit Two, she sensed a presence distinct from her own, with its own will.

Could that presence be my—

An alarm suddenly went off, and the siren lights began spinning. Everyone took off running.

The Magi's artificial voice came through the speakers. 《All sectors are entering lockdown. This is not a drill.》

But the Magi didn't state the reason for the lockdown or the category of the alarm.

《This message will repeat. All sectors are—》

With a deep, mechanical rumble, barrier walls of high-tensile steel began closing off sections of the HQ.

"It can't be!" Maya rushed to the elevator lobby, pushing her way through the crowd.

Asuka followed.

"Sorry," Maya said, "but the next one out is going directly to Cage Two!"

Her phone rang in the pocket of her lab coat.

《Chief Ibuki! Super Eva has suddenly gone unstable on the quantum level! Measurements show that its structure is becoming more and more distorted, and—》

So that had been the cause of the alarm. Maya interrupted, "Where's Shinji?"

《He's... Well, when we weren't looking, he...》

"Find him! He can't leave the Eva's side."

Together, they're one, Asuka repeated to herself. The answer to her question was happening right now.

"You need to enter Unit Two," Maya said.

"Shouldn't I help look for Shinji?"

"Part of your duty is to make sure we still *have* an Eva after this. Besides, if Super Eva self-destructs and splits the main island of Japan in half, you might survive inside Unit Two."

"It's that serious?"

"Before all this, there might have been someone—a presence—within Unit One. And if Shinji has assumed that role while still remaining a human being separate from the Eva, then he's living a double existence."

The elevator arrived, and the display above the doors indicated, *Direct to Cage Two.*

When the doors opened, Maya stepped in, immediately followed by a crowd wearing the same color security passes as she was, and Asuka lost sight of her.

The command center received the report from Cage Two, and the technicians began considering the worst-case scenario— if Super Eva's heart/extradimensional window completely broke down.

"What do they mean that Super Eva and Shinji's existence is attenuating?" Aoba asked.

"We can get the explanation later!" Misato shouted. "Inform the Japanese government that we're postponing the return of the evacuees. We need to figure out how well we can mitigate the worst-case outcome. I want to hear everyone's opinions."

《Cage Two to command. Chief Ibuki has just arrived.》

"Where's Asuka?"

《This is Asuka. I'm at my cage.》 She spoke over the sound of rustling clothes and her plugsuit decompressing.

Eva-02's status monitor switched to standby.

"Unit Two," Misato said, "I'm deploying you to Tokyo-3. Protect the city with your A.T. Field."

《That's crazy... Misato, where's Shinji?》

"We'll find him."

《At least send Rei up with Unit Zero.》

Asuka thought she might use this crisis to get Rei Trois out of confinement, but Misato had already decided to do just that.

"Is Rei...Trois still in the lab control room?" Misato asked.

"About that," replied one of Aoba's men, a technician on the lower deck. "Someone showed up at the lab with a visitor pass and made a request..."

A massive ring formed the outer edge of Nerv HQ. On the building's roof—called the Grand Deck—were several armored structures mounted on rails, which could be repositioned at will.

One such structure, currently located on the southwest side, held a hive of antenna towers. A small white figure was climbing the service staircase on one of the outermost towers. It was Shinji in a hospital gown.

"Well, they're all worked up."

Through a gentle breeze, alarms echoed back and forth between the buildings and the mountains along the caldera's inner rim.

In a strange way, the more hopeless the situation, the more a person could find beauty in the mundane. Just now, Shinji thought the wind felt nice.

How did everything end up like this? he wondered.

Within his chest, where his heart should have been, there was nothing.

His arteries still originated there, and his veins terminated there. His blood vessels, nerves, and other tissues all faded away at the border of the void.

A theoretical physicist Shinji had never met before—apparently an associate professor at the college Aoba had attended, though Shinji thought the man sounded shady all the same— explained it like this: The empty space, which no scanner could resolve, connected directly to Shinji's Eva, and through it, the pair shared a single heart.

It didn't make any sense.

The scientists had discovered a new mystery of the universe inside Shinji's body, but he had never asked for or wanted it.

To Shinji, it was as if Eva-01 had stolen his heart.

Then again, after being reconstructed by the Eva, am I really myself anymore?

Once he started thinking like that, he began to question if he had even been himself after the battle with Zeruel three years ago when his synchronization rate went so high he lost form and merged with the LCL.

He shook his head, trying to clear his mind. "They tell me that I'm not just connected with the Eva—we've completely merged on a quantum level."

He wasn't talking to himself. He had noticed Toji and Rei Trois climbing the metal stairs after him.

"If they're in this much of a panic," he added, "I guess it must be true."

Cage Two was located at the eleven o'clock position of the HQ's outer ring. The cage's partially destroyed roof began moving clockwise, and an adjacent anti-air structure slid after it to fill the gap.

Someone must have decided that this particular module would provide a better barrier should Super Eva self-destruct.

As the structure moved into place, it began dumping cage carts containing airtight and shockproof packages of guided missiles onto the Grand Deck. Meanwhile, its cannons thundered, firing ammunition into the empty sky to rid itself of everything explosive.

Toji reflexively covered his ears. "What happens if you move away from Super Eva?" he shouted.

"It gets unstable—no, wait, the word Maya used was 'uncertain.'"

"Huh? I can't hear you!"

"The Eva's existence becomes uncertain!" Shinji yelled. "It'll disappear!"

But Toji knew that the Eva wouldn't simply disappear. The S^2 Engine—or the heart, or whatever it was that he had helped pull the ropes to construct—would be unleashed. Toji didn't know exactly what would happen, but several terrible outcomes sprang to mind.

"But that's..." Toji said. "You know..."

He needed a moment to choose his words carefully. An unnatural silence fell over the Grand Deck as the anti-air module halted on the track and, for a moment, stopped firing.

The roof of Cage Two hadn't fully sealed, yet the structure was still.

Something had stopped it.

A hand thrust out from the cage.

Sparks flew from the wheels on the track, and the multi-ton anti-air module jolted and groaned as it was pushed aside.

Having brushed away the interloper, the hand grasped the rail. Arm muscles swelled, sending rumbles through the building as the Eva pulled up the rest of its body.

Super Eva leaped into the air, performing a somersault before landing. The ground shook, and the Eva began battering the anti-air structure with its fists.

The module had resumed firing its remaining ammunition, but Super Eva had inadvertently placed itself directly in its line of fire. The shells burst as they struck the Eva's body, scattering countless shards onto the Grand Deck that ricocheted as far as Tokyo-3.

"Cease fire!" Misato shouted. "Stop dumping the ammo! Stop it now!"

The technicians hurriedly shut down the module's cannons.

"Chief Ibuki, what's going on?"

The drumbeat of Super Eva pummeling the armored structure could be heard all the way down in the command center.

《Just as Asuka reported, the Eva has formed an A.T. Field in the exact same shape as its body. According to our best theories, an A.T. Field is the vessel of a conscious existence. If that's true, then what we're seeing is an idealized version of—》

"That's not what I'm asking!"

The anti-air module continued to sustain damage, but so far, the structure had held.

Super Eva was attacking haphazardly, and the impacts weren't focused on a single spot.

Anyone observing could easily tell... that the Eva was confused.

"I don't understand anything!" Shinji yelled, as Super Eva rampaged in the background. "I just want to go away—whoever I am!"

"Is that really how you feel?" Trois asked. The distant pounding underscored her question. "Unit One," she started to say and then corrected herself. "Super Eva is confused."

"It's supposed to do what I tell it, right? I willed it to come!"

"You're wrong," Trois said firmly. "The Eva doesn't belong to you—it's *another* you. It's a you that doesn't want to die and doesn't want to disappear."

With another loud rumble, a large shadow passed over the tower and blocked the sun.

What Ayanami said had angered Shinji, and Super Eva had responded, springing off the Grand Deck and leaping toward the tower. The trailing wind threatened to sweep Ayanami away, and she, Shinji, and Toji clung to the handrails as the ground shook, momentarily lifting their feet from the steps.

Standing behind Toji, Ayanami said, "Don't run from this. Accept that the Eva is also you. You can't give up," she pressed. "You're the one who made this world three years ago."

Before Shinji knew it, Super Eva was reaching for Ayanami from the tower's other side. The action was an impulse, a subconscious manifestation of Shinji's indignation at having the truth forced upon him.

Everyone felt that impulse now and then, anger followed by aggression. Most were capable of controlling or redirecting the urge to be violent. But for them, the impulse didn't manifest as an armored giant.

Toji placed himself directly in front of Ayanami.

The Eva's fingers froze in the air around the two of them as if stopped by a large, invisible sphere.

If Super Eva was the manifestation of Shinji's rage, then this sphere was his past trauma—and his inability to ever crush Toji again.

For the past three years, Toji had been aware of Shinji's guilt over Eva-01 having once crushed him in its grasp. And though he had expected this outcome, stepping into harm's way had been a gamble.

Toji slumped as the terror drained from his body.

"I thought I was gonna piss myself," he said.

Ayanami tried to support Toji from behind, but he was too heavy for her, and the two collapsed in a heap.

Shinji's anger immediately cooled. He cowered, burying his face in his hands as he realized what he had nearly done. He felt disgusted and horrified. It didn't matter that they were safe now. He had almost murdered Ayanami and Toji.

"You wanted to take Super Eva somewhere that there was no one else around, is that it?" Ayanami asked.

Shinji's head was still down.

"Ikari-kun," she said, "Try doing what I do."

Her suggestion was so unexpected that Shinji couldn't comprehend what she meant.

"Imitate me," she said. "What I do."

Shinji still didn't understand.

Scratching his head, Toji offered, "Ayanami thinks she can help you coexist with Super Eva. She's offering to teach you. What have you got to lose, Shinji? Give it a try."

Uncertain, Shinji looked to Ayanami. She nodded.

Ayanami didn't think of her offer as "teaching." The phrase simply hadn't entered her mind. It was a sequence she'd never followed before—taking actions, gaining experience, then passing her knowledge on to others.

"What you do is...recognize that there's another you outside of yourself," Ayanami explained.

"Huh?" Shinji's eyes were puffy.

Ayanami thought for a moment. How would someone approach this? "Asuka would say something like, 'I'm a pro at having more than one of me.'"

"Ah..." She was talking about the mental mirror that connected the four Ayanamis. Though at the moment—

"But your connection is broken," he blurted. "You're not a pro."

Then Shinji fell silent because Ayanami smiled faintly, reminding him of the presence he'd once felt inside his Eva. She had that effect on him more and more as the years went by, and he wasn't sure how to react.

It felt wrong to equate the two women.

"Toji, I'm sorry," Shinji said, unable to meet his friend's eyes.

But Toji was evidently also feeling self-conscious, and he refused to use Shinji's guilt against him. "It's fine," Toji said. "Ayanami-sensei, would you continue your lesson?"

"Repeat after me," she said. "Ikari the human can see Ikari the Eva."

She paused, and he repeated the words, sounding like a student in a foreign language class.

"Me the human can see...me the Eva."

"Ikari-kun the Eva's eyes are watching Ikari-kun the human."

"Me the Eva's eyes are...watching me the human."

That was all they said, but those few words were like a spell awakening Shinji to his ability.

Toji watched as the anger drained from Super Eva's shoulders, and the giant's pent-up energy evaporated. Its muscles relaxed, and the shrill noise of straining metal faded. The giant was still.

Ayanami Rei Trois spoke.

"I was one person as four. Now I'm as three, and I can't maintain a connection with two of them. Part of myself is missing... and it feels terrible. Ikari-kun, don't lose any part of who you are."

"Okay," Shinji said.

Super Eva towered above them.

Its eyes had remained open since the fight against the Angel Carrier, but now the visor slowly lowered over them.

"Command center, this is Ibuki."

Maya and a crowd of white-coated scientists had surrounded them at a distance. They were accompanied by security officers, whose rifles were pointed at Shinji's head.

"Silence the alarm," Maya said. "The Eva has stabilized...for now."

At once, the gun barrels lowered.

"It's falling!" someone shouted. "Brace for impact!"

The noise and vibrations returned as Super Eva swayed and then sank to its knees.

In the aftermath, the only sound was the beating of the giant's heart.

Rei Trois turned her head. "Someone...is watching."

She looked up. The midday moon shone bright in the sky.

CHAPTER 14

▷ ——————————— **A DARK RIVER**

FAR AWAY, the fugitive Ayanami—Rei Quatre—opened her eyes with a start.

She had gained some measure of consciousness, though her sense of self was still unstable, stuck in a cycle of waking and submerging—now interrupted by searing pain.

She felt like she was burning up from the inside, and she didn't know why.

Her breath caught. She whimpered.

I'm scared.

Without warning, she found herself at the mercy of a feeling no version of Ayanami Rei had ever truly experienced—terror.

A delayed realization accompanied this terror—that she and her Eva were drifting through an unfamiliar, pitch-black space.

She had no way of knowing where she was. All her Eva's sensors read zero. Unable to process the situation, she began to panic.

As her body burned, she felt as though she were being washed away into a vast river at the bottom of the earth.

She clutched her chest.

The black heat flowed deep inside of her and began climbing its way into her brain, as if to say, *I found you.*

S-stop!

Her pulse thundered in her ears.

The heat was forcing information into her brain.

Her shared memories with the other Ayanamis tumbled around her mind, disjointed.

The heat pieced together words, and her lips opened by a will that was not her own.

"I...won't allow it! I won't allow it to exist!"

As she spoke, unbidden, a vision came to Quatre. For the first time, she saw Shinji's new Eva.

UNFORGIVABLE

*P*ICTURE YOURSELF *grabbing an object. Then grab it for real.*
    With this simple exercise, Shinji trained himself to recognize where his body ended and his Eva's body began. Through repetition, Rei Trois taught Shinji how to coexist among multiple selves. After two weeks of drilling, day in and day out, he had finally begun to catch on.

Temporary living quarters had been set up for him on the side of Cage Two's control room.

Today, he was moving out.

Once his perception of his selves had been fixed in place, Shinji was able to travel away from Super Eva without the giant destabilizing—so long as he stayed within the caldera that contained Tokyo-3 and Lake Ashi.

This would be the last day he and Rei Trois sat across from each other for one-on-one training, which, even after so many sessions, he still attended with some reluctance.

Every now and then, Asuka and Toji came by to joke around, but most of the time, he was alone with Rei. The training resembled a mother teaching her child proper behavior.

Which was exactly how Shinji least wanted to think of Rei.

Ayanami is Ayanami, Shinji told himself, doing his best to remain rational. On the whole, it had worked, and the training had gone more smoothly than he'd expected.

"Let's do one last review," Rei Trois said. "People can read books and drink tea at the same time because we hold infinite layers in our consciousness."

But theory was one thing. Being conscious of several discrete actions at once was a lot more complicated.

"It's incredible that you've been able to do this with so many selves," Shinji said.

"It's not as different as you might think, Ikari-kun. After all, between you and Super Eva, you have four arms, so—"

Seated in a metal folding chair across from Shinji, Rei Trois stopped speaking mid-sentence.

Her eyes became unfocused, as if she were looking somewhere far beyond him.

"Ayanami?"

"You who have failed your parts...depart from the stage at once."

Shinji gaped at her. "Um...what?"

Her eyes remained unfocused as she reached for Shinji with both arms.

Reflexively, Shinji retreated as far back as the chair would allow, its metal feet scraping against the floor.

Ayanami's hands felt Shinji's chest, as if they were searching for something.

"Ah! Hey," Shinji sputtered. "What are you doing?"

Is this part of the training? Oh... Oh, no!

Shinji had grown agitated, and he sensed Super Eva beginning to stir.

Quickly, he tried to refocus his thoughts.

Be aware of every movement. Be aware. My body isn't moving, but my heart is beating fast.

Behind him, on the other side of a blast-resistant wall, Super Eva's heart beat.

My heart! Is Ayanami searching for my heart?

Shinji shuddered. He lifted Ayanami's pale, crawling fingers off his chest.

"That heartbeat," she intoned, "must not be."

"Ayanami?"

Wham! There was a tremendous rumble, and Shinji's water cup danced across the nearby table.

Was it an earthquake? *If it was, we wouldn't feel it. This building is on a floating foundation.*

Wham! Another rumble, and the cup toppled over.

"What are those shocks?" Shinji asked. "Maybe we should get out of here, Trois."

"The world," Ayanami said, "will be reborn."

The tremor sounded as if though it were coming from far away. The crew outside the HQ—and the citizens, freshly returned to Tokyo-3—looked up instinctively to the crescent moon.

The alarm sounded, and the primary staff were summoned to the command center—but not because of the rumbles.

It happened during the shift change from day to night. Misato had been headed to her personal quarters, but now she returned to her station where a technician filled her in.

"There's an abnormality with the orbital Series-0.0 Units. Cinq and Six are—"

"Put their voices on speaker!" Misato ordered. "What happened? I thought we put them to sleep."

"Yes, we had slowed their metabolisms, and they were in a state of hibernation, until suddenly..."

The pilots of the two remaining orbiting Evas appeared on the screen. Six, unlike the other clones, had the appearance of a young child—maybe five or six years old. Their lips were faintly moving. When the volume was turned up, they intoned in unison.

《Transgression... You who have failed your parts... Depart from the stage at once.》

The building quaked.

The command center shook, and the computer stations rattled and creaked.

Irritated, Misato asked, "Has anyone figured out where these tremors are coming from?"

"We...haven't," Aoba said, bewildered on the middle deck. The meteorologists on the lower deck looked just as confused. "It's happening everywhere in the world."

"What do you mean everywhere?"

The main screen filled with seismographic data from sensor nodes in Europe, Asia, North America, South America, Australia, and every ocean, timestamped in UTC. The data was layered on top of itself and then filtered for noise, leaving one steady pulse.

Aoba pointed at the screen. "We're getting measurements from all over the globe. And there's no time lag. When we control for secondary reflections and propagating vibrations, all that's left is a longitudinal wave of equal magnitude."

"That's impossible!"

"You're not wrong," Aoba said. "The vibration doesn't adhere to planetary physics."

Hyuga followed up with a report on the troubles in orbit.

"Commander Katsuragi, Cinq and Six's brain waves are in synchronization. This pattern is something we've never seen before, but both appear to be in the subservient role."

Are they both responding to the same stimulus? Misato wondered. *Has the Ayanamis' mental mirroring been restored? If so, then who is controlling them?*

"Where's Ayanami Trois?" Misato asked.

Maya's voice came through the display. 《Trois isn't behind this.》

By this time, Shinji had informed the chief scientist of Rei Trois' abnormal behavior, and Maya had quickly hooked her into a brain activity monitor.

《Her alpha waves have increased. Trois isn't making them do this—she's also being controlled.》

"And in the chief scientist's opinion, what the hell is going on?"

《Something is taking over these girls.》

"Like a kind of...mental contamination? Ayanami Quatre is still missing. Could she be the instigator?"

《I've never seen these brain patterns before. They're very far from normal for a human. If this was Quatre's doing, I'd know.》

Misato sighed. "In other words, I'm wrong."

《Maybe not entirely. It's possible that Quatre was corrupted by some other entity, and the corruption is spreading to Trois, Cinq, and Six.》

Wham! Another tremor.

"We're receiving an urgent report from the air surveillance station!" Hyuga interjected.

"What is with this day?" Misato grumbled.

The window on the main display was replaced by an image dotted with stars.

"It's an aberration in the primary surveillance sector on the moon," Hyuga explained, "designated Relic One."

"What?!"

Of everything that had happened so far, nothing could have been more unthinkable.

Every time the moon climbed the sky over Nerv HQ, the main tower's telescope tracked the same target on its surface—an object that remained under strict, constant surveillance by eyes all over the globe.

The Lance of Longinus.

The lance recently stolen from Eva-02 was a copy of the mass-production Evas had carried into the Battle at Nerv HQ.

Rei's Eva-00 had thrown the original lance at the Angel Arael. After destroying the Angel, the lance had escaped Earth's gravity and planted itself in the Sea of Crises, where it had been stuck ever since.

The lance's lunar impact had created the Longinus Crater.

For three years, the lance had been sticking out of the ground at the center of a circular scar.

But not anymore.

"What is that thing?!" Misato asked.

A massive arm held the double helix lance aloft.

The arm was attached to a giant wearing black armor.

The giant swung its arm and struck the moon's surface with the butt of the lance.

Wham!

They'd found the source of the tremors.

"Now hold on," Misato said. "This can't be right! Vibrations from the moon can't travel all the way here."

Every time this massive, humanoid figure struck the surface of the moon, the vibrations traveled through space, where no sound should have been able to carry.

Wham!

The Ayanamis spoke.

《You who have failed your parts...depart from the stage at once.》

"Did that thing do this to Ayanami?" Misato said as Shinji entered the command center, pushing Rei Trois in a wheelchair. Maya, the chief scientist, followed them.

Rei Trois' eyes were vacant, and her arms had been strapped to the chair's armrests.

Her mouth moved in unison with the two remote Ayanamis on the main screen.

《From the great flood...the stage will be reborn...as many times as needed until the project is complete.》

"The project?" Misato repeated.

"The UN Security Council has authorized the use of Aten's Hammer," Hyuga announced.

Misato looked surprised. "That was fast."

Aten's Hammer was the watchdog over the Lance of Longinus. The anti-Angel weapon—essentially a large rock with a rocket strapped to it—had been placed at the L_2 Lagrangian point on the far side of the moon, where centripetal force and gravity reached an equilibrium. Add to that its nuclear pulse engines, and Aten's Hammer could build up tremendous kinetic energy.

As Nerv Japan asserted its independence, the United Nations, as the only organization with authority over Nerv, had constructed Aten's Hammer so that they could have an Angel extermination system under their direct control without having to rely on Nerv.

Whatever the UN's public justification, the weapon's true purpose was generally assumed to be preventing Nerv from reclaiming the lance. But events had now directed the weapon against an enemy of humanity.

Fast? Misato thought ruefully. *There's nothing fast about this. We've been preparing for three years. And now we're being beaten to the punch by the UN!*

No... That's now how I should be thinking. I don't care who takes responsibility so long as the enemy is defeated.

Whether or not this new entity's intentions were hostile, once it had put its hand on the lance, the matter was moot.

Impatient, Misato asked a question to which she already knew the answer. "Can't we send out the Series-0.0 Evas?"

"Not in their current state," Maya said. "If we increase their sedatives and force them back into a deep sleep, then we could try waking them back up, and maybe..."

But there was no guarantee they would reawaken in any kind of normal state. And even if they did, there wasn't enough time.

The image on the main screen was replaced by a sharper one with less atmospheric distortion.

"This is the feed from Mauna Kea in Hawaii," a technician announced.

The black figure still stood on the moon's surface.

Judging by the lance's length, the giant appeared to be a third again as tall as an Evangelion.

Behind it, two plates rose from the moon's surface, taller even than the giant. A thin, glowing ring hung in the air behind its head. The giant's heavy black armor covered every inch of its body, and here and there across the armor's surface, red patterns glowed.

Unprompted, the Magi system said, "Warning. The library indicates several matching shapes associated with previously identified hostile entities."

《The scales!》 Asuka interjected from Eva-02. 《Those things were on the Angel Carriers, too! Shinji, you saw them, didn't you? Is this the bastard that sent the Carrier to steal my lance?》

Shrinking from Asuka's indignant yelling, Shinji looked up at the main display with trepidation. "How do we know that's... an enemy?"

A fair distance away, his heart beat, and Shinji's body shivered.

As if responding to the sound, the Ayanamis spoke in unison, two on the screen and one behind him, surrounding Shinji with their words.

《That pulse...must not be written...on the parchment of time.》

Wham!

The black giant struck the far-off moon with the Lance of Longinus.

Shinji gulped. Beads of sweat had appeared on his throat. All eyes in the command center were on him.

《Wow.》 Asuka frowned. 《I think it's calling you out.》

"So...an enemy then." Shinji sounded disconcerted.

Asuka groaned. 《You're so pathetic. You could at least try and come up with a comeback.》

"Huh?"

《What I mean is, we need to find out if this...telephone our blue-haired ladies are connected to works both ways!》

If the Ayanamis were acting as a proxy for the black giant, could Nerv talk to it through them?

"Chief Ibuki?" Misato asked.

Maya nodded to indicate the idea was possible.

The chief scientist took a seat at an auxiliary station and switched the terminal on. But then she realized she'd forgotten something she needed and clicked her tongue.

"Suzuhara, of the above-ground support staff, entering the command center."

Toji appeared from the elevator with Maya's cell phone in his outstretched hand.

"Special delivery," he said. "Whoa! What the heck is that thing?"

Shinji turned to Rei Trois in her wheelchair and asked, "What do you want from me?"

《I seek...for the actor who invited failure...to exit the stage.》

A flurry of glowing letters raced across the display.

The Magi system was absorbing everything the Ayanamis said, and with each new word, the AI performed tens of thousands of comparative analyses.

《So that the ark...can carry the remaining actors...to the new stage.》

The Magi system narrowed its focus to religious mythologies. *The end of days. Eschaton.* Words from religious literature regarding the end of the world remained on the screen rather than disappearing.

In hushed tones, a technician said, "Domine, quo vadis?"

Lord, where are you going?

"What god would look like *that?*" Misato asked.

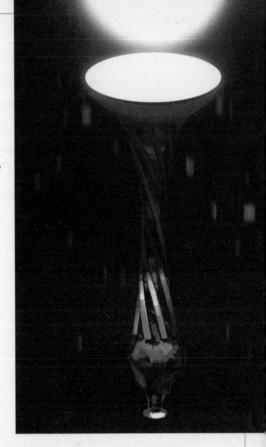

Far away on the moon, a never-before-seen spectacle had begun, leaving everyone in the command center with their mouths hanging open.

The Lance of Longinus's double helix was unwinding.

The crew in the command center had about a second to stare at the screen in stunned silence before the air shook.

"Gravitational waves," Maya announced. "The lance's helix has been theorized to contain folded threads of enormous energy. Is that what we're seeing now?"

The unwound helix became a single, radiant line. The black giant held it aloft and then threw the shining object toward the Earth.

As if synchronized with the giant's movement, Rei Trois suddenly tore her right arm free from its restraints.

The guard nearest to her was slow to react, and Trois spilled out of her chair, tipping it over. She fell toward Shinji, who caught her by the shoulders. Still in the restraint, her left arm bent—the bones creaking, threatening to break—but she paid no attention and put her free hand on Shinji's chest.

《The Earth will be within the ring...》 the Ayanamis intoned. 《Disconnected from the outside...until the original sin is undone.》

"The original sin?" Shinji asked.

《The Human...Instrumentality...Project.》

In the next instant, Shinji's back was brightly illuminated.

On the main screen, a great flash of light appeared on the surface of the moon.

The video feeds from multiple telescopes all blanked out, and the ones from the moon's orbital satellites became garbled with digital noise. The cameras switched to high-density filters, revealing a giant, upside-down, cone-shaped plume of smoke rising from the moon and swallowing the giant figure.

Aten's Hammer had landed.

The 6,100-ton rock had been chosen from the Aten asteroid group.

Tritium-pellet nuclear pulse engines had propelled the asteroid from its station at the L_2 Lagrangian point 60,000 kilometers beyond the far side of the moon. The rock struck at a speed of over 100 kilometers per second, resulting in a staggering 1.25-gigaton explosion.

The crescent moon, partially lit by the sun, suddenly became as bright as a full moon.

Had the black giant been defeated? The rising cloud obscured it from view. But the Ayanamis continued to speak.

《Withdraw, you who didn't do what must be done... Leave the stage with haste... The Earth proceeds to a new stage... Events will repeat...from the original sin... Next time, the world will be set free.》

The giant vanished into the particulate cloud the explosion had sent into the silent darkness.

But the crisis wasn't over. The Lance of Longinus continued its flight through the void.

"Calculate the lance's trajectory," Misato commanded

"I'm trying, but... Damn it!" Aoba cursed. "The hammer's generating too much background noise."

Despite the interference, the computers were soon able to lock on to the weapon.

Aoba straightened in his chair. "The lance is on course to strike Earth in approximately... Wait, how is it still accelerating? I need to see a different wavelength. Send over the data from Nobeyama."

With moondust cascading across the main screen at his back, Toji held the wheelchair steady as Shinji helped Trois back into it.

An enemy in humanoid form, Misato thought.

"It's just like an Eva," a technician said softly.

But Misato heard. *And I don't think it's just one or two of us thinking the exact same thing.*

She adjusted her microphone and spoke to all decks of the command center.

"I'm naming that black-armored thing Armaros. Revise all documents going back to its first sighting."

Toji and Shinji looked puzzled, as if to say, *Why? It's already gone.*

They didn't understand information's insidious ability to spread.

"The intelligence department will begin steering and managing external information," Misato said. "By naming it after a fallen angel, we will blot out any association of our enemy with the Evangelions."

"Ikari-kun, I..." Rei Trois' bizarre, trance-like state had lifted. She was trembling, and her familiar expression had returned.

Shinji was beginning to wonder if Armaros' mental interference had gone away. But just then, the two orbiting Ayanamis spoke.

《I am not you.》

《You are different from me.》

Their words tumbled out, like a dam had burst.

《I refuse to yield my decisions to the bigger me.》

《I won't decide for the me whose image is mixed with my own.》

Trois looked frightened.

《I am me.》

《I, too, am me.》

Have the two Ayanamis in the orbital Series-0.0 Evas awakened? Misato asked herself. *If the giant's influence has left them, then...*

She gave an order. "Reactivate Units Cinq and Six, and do it fast!"

"I...can't reach them. Chief Ibuki?"

"The three girls aren't able to get their thoughts in sync," Maya said, "but this..." She began opening windows showing Cinq's and Six's vital signs and brain activity. "This doesn't match the expected deviation from an interrupted mental link."

"Maya," Misato responded, "keep the explanations brief. We need to ready a counterattack against the Lance of Longinus as quickly as possible."

《I am not any other person.》

《Other people aren't me.》

The pair weren't speaking just for the sake of it—they seemed to be speaking to one person, the primary Rei, Number Trois.

《I am different from my indistinct you. My name is Number Cinq.》

《I am watching my unseeable you from outside myself. I am Number Six.》

Cinq and Six were referring to Trois in the second person, even though the three of them were one self. Trois felt their eyes upon her, and her body stiffened.

"Why are you calling me a 'you'?" Trois covered her ears with her hands. "You *are* me. So why can't I find you...me...in myself?"

Maya sensed danger.

"Shinji, wheel Trois back into her room at once. I'll join you soon."

Maya approached Misato and whispered into her ear. "This isn't the kind of de-sync that comes from an interrupted connection. They are actively pushing her out and trying to construct their own individuality."

"What are you talking about?"

"It's possible that a sense of self has awakened within Number Cinq and Number Six—like Number Quatre."

Misato pounded her fist against her terminal. *Now of all times!*

Toji started to leave with Shinji and Trois, but Maya stopped him.

"Suzuhara-kun, I need you on that auxiliary station to relay Cinq and Six's status to me in the control room."

"What?! I-I can't do that."

Toji shook his head emphatically, but Maya's request hadn't been arbitrary. Having been trained as a pilot, Toji was accustomed to the nature of communications in the command center. He'd even practiced guiding pilots. But that had been three years ago.

"Please," Maya said. "Right now, we have one person who is turning into three. I can't handle this by myself."

She disappeared into the elevator.

A young technician at a communications station on the lower deck noticed a change in the incoming requests.

"I'm getting repeated inquiries from national observatories and defense organizations about the lance's length," she reported to Aoba, her commanding officer.

But it was Hyuga, in the seat next to Aoba, who responded. "So, it really *is* getting longer!"

"What?!"

Hyuga switched his comms channel to the top deck. "Commander, the lance has lengthened. We didn't know for sure until now. We've had difficulty getting reliable measurements while the weapon is heading toward us. I thought we'd been getting erroneous readings, but...the data indicates the lance is 1,200 meters long."

All sense has fled, Misato thought. This latest development left her no closer to guessing their enemy's intention, and it only strengthened her dread.

"The Lance of Longinus has been growing longer," she muttered to herself.

Is it lengthening still?

Upon reaching eighty kilometers per second, the lance's acceleration began to slow. At ninety, its velocity remained constant. At that speed, it would arrive at Earth within an hour.

"The lance's current length is 1,400 meters," Hyuga reported.

The weapon's acceleration might have stopped, but it continued to lengthen.

"Has there been any change in the lance's trajectory?" Misato asked.

"None." Hyuga sounded apologetic. "It's still on course for a direct hit."

Whatever calculations Armaros had made before the throw,

any mid-flight changes to the lance's speed or mass should have altered its trajectory. And yet, the Lance of Longinus continued toward the Earth, just as it had the moment it had been thrown.

"It's like the lance *wants* to hit the Earth," Misato said. "It's absurd."

"Attention!" Hyuga called. "Russian attack satellites have begun firing lasers at the lance."

The lance was now visible in the sky as a bar of light approaching the Earth. Small flashes added to the weapon's radiance.

Hyuga continued, "And the UN Secretariat is saying they're sending us a strategic advisor."

Misato shook her head. "There's no chance a UNTRP military attaché will get here before the lance does!"

The UN was deeply skeptical that Nerv's anti-Angel search-and-destroy network was indeed inoperative.

"The lance is undamaged, and its trajectory remains steady," Hyuga reported. "I repeat, no change has been detected in the lance's trajectory."

Rei Trois slept on the adjustable bed in the laboratory control room.

The sedative had taken effect. Until moments ago, she had been trembling and clutching at the bedsheets.

Shinji received the order to activate Super Eva. Given how forcefully Armaros had denounced the Eva's heart, Misato was concerned that the giant might have targeted it with the lance.

On his way out the door, Shinji turned. "Maya-san, will Trois be..."

"Her mental link wasn't merely severed this time. Cinq and Six cast her out. What would it feel like if your hands one day said, 'We're not you,' and left?"

On the desk, the intercom chimed.

《Maya-san, Six is...》

It was Toji, and his voice was desperate. The command center sounded like it was in disarray.

"What happened?" Maya asked.

《She's not listening to a word I say. She's confused. She started crying.》

Faintly in the background, a child's voice wailed.

"What about Cinq?"

《She increased the dosage of her own sedative and put herself into an even deeper sleep. Hyuga-san thinks that Cinq is having trouble processing her transformation, that she knocked herself out before she had a breakdown.》

Well now, Maya thought, *Cinq ran away. But Six hasn't.*

"The crying might be a good sign. Sometimes that can work like an emergency pressure-release valve. Do what you can to help her through it."

Now was the time for empathy.

After hanging up, Toji said, with exasperation, "Help her through it?"

Seriously?

《Waaaah!》

Six's wailing filled the command center, where technicians were attempting to calculate the Lance of Longinus's impact point.

One of them started a report. "The lance's angle of incidence is—"

《Waaaaaah!》

"Can't somebody switch off the sound from orbital control?!" An operative complained from another station.

"Divert communications from Unit Six to the top deck auxiliary station," Hyuga said.

Toji was starting to feel more and more like an air traffic controller.

"If the Russian laser satellites are still operational, have them send us their data." Misato said into a receiver. "What do you mean 'they refuse?' It's *top secret?!*"

She was probably talking to the UN. A whole lot of angry shouting came from the other end of the line.

《Waaaaaaa—》

Click.

Toji rerouted Six's sound so that it only came through his headset.

"Hey, would you stop crying? Please?"

It was strange. Toji had been told that all the Ayanamis shared the same memories.

When he'd seen them in person, back before they were launched into orbit, they moved and spoke identically to Trois

even though their physical bodies were different. Given this previous experience, speaking with Six like this felt...unreal.

Toji sighed. "So...you're an Ayanami, right? Could you maybe try being quiet and not saying anything, like Trois?"

Six sobbed. "I'm Six, not Trois!"

Oh? Toji thought. *Treating her like Trois touched a nerve.*

"Oh, yeah? So you've developed a...sense of self, or something like that? Well, in that case..."

Toji put on the biggest smile he could.

"Congratulations."

The line went silent. After a long pause, she responded.

《Congratulations?》 Another short sob. But at least it didn't lead to more wails. 《For what, Suzuhara Toji?》

Is this really Ayanami?

She sounds like my sister, only even younger.

The distraction seemed to have worked, like he'd moved a toy from one hand to the other and the first hand was immediately forgotten.

But if the copies start with the same knowledge and thoughts, shouldn't they end with identical results?

Toji was about to learn that Six wasn't just any child. He sent the Lance of Longinus's data to her Series-0.0 Eva, and this time, the command went through. The Eva's primary FSB ignited.

Six shrieked.

She wasn't completely terrified anymore, but her mental state was still unstable.

Toji didn't understand it at the time, but Six had begun accepting HQ's commands not out of a sense of duty but rather out of her desire—and inability—to find mental stability. With no way to process what she was experiencing, she chose external action over internal reflection.

The FSB's flares formed an inverted cross nearly five times the height of the Eva. In Brazil, on the opposite side of the world, an astronomical observatory captured images of the flames burning in the sky.

In the command center, a technician announced, "Six's Eva has broken orbit and is switching to a new trajectory. I repeat, Six's Eva has..."

The telemetry data confirmed that the Series-0.0 Eva had begun moving to intercept the Lance of Longinus.

Hyuga let out a small gasp of surprise.

How did you do it, Toji?

On the Eva's status monitor, the readings were still all over the map, but they were all rising.

In fact, they were rising too quickly. Guided by its pilot's mental disarray, the S² Engine's power output spiked from normal combat levels to levels the Eva could only handle for a short time.

Six screamed.

With nowhere else for the energy to go, the engine's release valve vented a blast of firefly-like particles into outer space.

Six's scream seemed to offer the same release. Her breathing and heartbeat were racing.

"Unit Six," Misato said, "is she going to make it?"

She was relieved that Six was moving to intercept the lance, but she still felt uneasy. *Why would Armaros throw it at the Earth? Is this some kind of attack?* She couldn't read her enemy's intent.

Even with so many unknowns, the UN Security Council—currently in an emergency session—was urging Nerv Japan to alter the lance's trajectory. The weapon held enormous gravitational energy, and its impact would almost certainly cause devastation.

Misato turned to Toji in the support station.

"You're a lifesaver. Thank you, Suzuhara-kun."

Toji lifted his hands from his terminal as if to say, *My work here is done.*

But he still wasn't seeing signs of stability in Six, and the lance certainly wouldn't wait for them to appear.

"We've recalculated the predicted impact location," a technician announced. "USA. West Coast. San José."

"Hyuga-kun, send the gamma-ray laser cannon authorization code to Six's Eva," Misato commanded. "Six! I need you to make a concentrated attack on the Lance of Longinus. The goal is to alter its course."

Six grunted. Her eyelids fluttered as if she were having trouble focusing her vision. "Gamma-ray laser cannon, activation sequence initiating."

Toji monitored her brain waves. The pattern showed heightened levels of noise—much higher and she'd risk losing consciousness. The mental strain was clearly taking a toll on her recently awakened ego. It was painful for Toji to watch.

Hyuga continued to update her on the situation.

"Six, you're on the far side of the Earth from the lance. It will crest the horizon in 740 seconds."

《This is Six. Acknowledged.》 Another weak sob.

By the time Six acquired line of sight with the lance, the weapon would be within 30,000 kilometers of Earth.

Misato watched the seconds tick down. "There won't be time for her to make another orbit. This is our only chance."

The external S^2 Engine's roar rumbled through the Eva's body and into Six's ears.

《This... This isn't fun. What's there to congratulate?》

The blue mass of the Earth passed under her feet with tremendous speed.

《Shinji in Super Eva to Hakone command. I'm nearing the former Mount Kami.》

"This is Hakone command," Hyuga replied. "Acknowledged. We anticipate the lance might change trajectory, like a guided missile. Stay on your guard."

《This is Asuka in Unit Two. I've arrived at the Mount Komagatake sniping post. I'm equipped with a positron rifle. I can hit the lance if it drops into low orbit.》

"If it comes to that," Misato said, "we'll be counting on you."

"I'm transferring the meteorologists' latest data on gamma ray refraction in the ionosphere," Hyuga said.

"The lance will crest the horizon in 405 seconds!"

As tensions rose in the command center, Six called out for Toji.

《Suzuhara Toji, are you there? Is everyone...》 She sobbed. 《Is everyone this lonely?》

"You can do this," Toji said. "If you're feeling lonely, then we'll just have to cheer you up. Okay?"

"The lance is entering your line of fire," Misato said. "Six! Skim your laser across the upper atmosphere and hit the tip of it!"

The distances involved were no longer astronomical. The Eva and the lance were about to meet.

The lance's trajectory had already been calculated by the Eva's targeting system. All that was left was for Six to squeeze the trigger.

A blip had appeared on her screen, just at the edge of the round horizon, when suddenly, blindingly bright flashes appeared, one after another, in front of her Eva.

Six screamed.

"N_2 outer-space depth charges!" Hyuga shouted.

Misato stood. "Which country did that?! Six, are you there?"

Six's Eva had immediately applied filtering to the sudden brightness—though the entry plug's virtual display would never project enough light to burn her retinas—but the shock of this unexpected visual stimulus still momentarily disoriented her.

Because of that, she was late to notice.

Whether or not the N_2 depth charges were to blame, when the Lance of Longinus emerged from the explosions, it was hurtling straight toward Six's Eva.

Six yelped, and her small hand squeezed the trigger.

All at once, her Eva's capacitors released a massive amount of electricity.

The 1,900-gigawatt gamma-ray laser surged out from the long cannon.

As the laser grazed the top of the ionosphere, a hazy aurora appeared.

A direct hit!

An intense, rainbow-colored flash diffused outward.

But the lance's course remained steady.

Six brought up the targeting reticule, focused, and fired again.

Another direct hit!

But the lance kept flying toward her.

Six screamed.

Traveling at 90 kilometers per second, the lance closed the gap in moments.

All Six could think to do was shoot again.

《Six!》 Toji shouted. 《Get out of the way!》

Her limbs reacted immediately. Cameras on the ground saw the lance's beam of light pierce the Eva's cross-shaped FSB flares.

《Six!》 Toji cried out.

She had just barely dodged.

The Lance of Longinus slipped past her Eva like an oncoming train on adjacent tracks.

Still screaming, Six lowered her orbit and continued firing her laser as long as she could.

Her aim held true, and each time the laser struck the lance, a cascade of rainbow-colored particles fell to the Earth.

The sight was truly beautiful.

No matter how hard Six pushed her S² Engine, the capacitors eventually drained to the point where they couldn't power

the gamma-ray laser cannon's nuclear excitement unit.

"Six, cease fire!" Hyuga said. "We need to assess the effect of your attacks."

But Six kept targeting the lance.

"Six!" Toji couldn't help but interject. "It's gone. Stop!"

Electromagnetic interference from the laser canon distorted the image of her entry plug. Six released her trembling hand from the trigger, and her small shoulders rose and fell.

《Tell me, Toji,》 she said, out of breath, 《Congratulations... for what?》

Toji took a moment to think. She was asking in earnest, and he couldn't respond with anything flippant.

After the second Rei perished in the battle with Armisael three years ago, Trois had become Ayanami Rei.

Ayanami didn't want any other children to be turned into Eva pilots. Sharing her soul among four of her selves was a compromise she'd made with Nerv's military.

While Ayanami had split herself to create Quatre, Cinq, and Six, in a practical sense, the three were mere tools—weapons of war. If someone like that achieved self-awareness, could Toji unequivocally say, "Hey, good for you"?

《The others aren't with me now. I can't hear their voices. But I don't want to go back. Nothing makes sense!》

"This is about becoming your own person, right? That's something to applaud, but it won't be easy."

《What's that supposed to mean?》

Toji scratched his head. 《It's a milestone. Like a birthday. Maybe we should celebrate later."

《A birthday...》

If this was to be the first day of her new life, then maybe he was right.

During Armaros' attack, the people of the world had looked to the skies with worry. But more than an hour of calm had now followed the tremors. Hardly anyone noticed the lance's quiet flight across 38,000 kilometers of space. Unable to maintain a state of panic, the people had returned to their normal routines.

As the lance approached, the various governments of the world had been frozen with indecision. A few amateur astronomers had noticed the phenomenon and gotten worked up online, but the vast majority of people hadn't been concerned.

When Six fired at the Lance of Longinus, the impact had created violent but resplendent bursts of light.

From Northern Africa to Europe to Russia, the soft, rainbow-colored particles fell. Those outdoors who were touched by the light—some 1.9 million people—instantly turned to pillars of salt and crumbled.

Horaki Hikari was out shopping with her sisters in a small town in Germany.

She'd been on vacation in Australia when Nerv Germany asked her to come work for them.

She'd been surprised by the offer, but Nerv Japan had given their consent for a short-term contract. The rest had depended on her family. For her own part, Hikari was curious to see where Asuka had been raised.

If Asuka knew what I was doing here, I bet she'd be surprised.

Everyone at Nerv Germany was so nice.

Wherever she wanted to go, work-related or not, they furnished her with a guide and a luxury car.

Tonight, as with many other nights, she'd gone out into town. The sunset was romantic.

"Wow! Look at the sky," her older sister said, having just stepped out of the car to enter the restaurant where they had a dinner reservation. "It's like an aurora."

With those as her last words, she stood beneath the beautiful, majestic light and turned into a pillar of salt.

Screams started coming from all directions.

Hikari sprang out of the car toward her sister. In an instant, her bodyguards realized what was happening and piled on top of her like a heap of heavy winter coats. Every single one of them turned to salt as well.

Within Eva-02, at the Mount Komagatake sniping post inside the Hakone caldera, Asuka whispered, "Hikari? Hikari is somewhere crying..."

She wore a bewildered expression, like a cat who'd woken herself up by meowing in her sleep.

Where did that thought come from?

She felt a low tremor and made a small, startled noise.

《Is that an earthquake?》 Shinji asked from inside Super Eva. He'd felt it, too.

The tremor was weak, but it continued for a long time.

At their respective stations, both Evas crouched down.

Evangelions were hard to knock over while in operation, but on standby, more caution was required. By maintaining four points of contact with the ground—the tips of both feet and the two knee shields—they could keep their center of gravity low.

Posed as if in prayer, the two giants waited for the tremor to subside.

《Command center to all personnel. The Lance of Longinus may have entered a polar orbit at 20,000 kilometers.》

《What's a polar orbit?》 Shinji asked.

"A north-south orbit," Asuka explained. "Passes over the poles,"

《This is the command center.》 It was Hyuga. 《Be on your guard. The lance is passing you to the southwest.》

A thread of light passed over the southwestern ridge of the caldera's outer ring, heading toward the Gotemba area in the northwest.

The Lance of Longinus didn't stick to the polar orbit. Maintaining its altitude at 20,000 kilometers, the lance gradually changed the inclination of its orbit and continued circling the Earth, as if winding a ball of yarn.

At roughly the same time, the Earth's crust suddenly became active, and earthquakes sprang up all over the world.

It only took a few days for humanity to discover that the Earth was beginning to shrink. The decreased gravity caused GPS systems to lose accuracy, and communications satellites deviated from their orbits and dropped their connections.

The Lance of Longinus was compressing the planet.

Soon, the Earth could no longer contain the pressure, and its mass began finding ways to escape.

NEON GENESIS
EVANGELION ANIMA

CHAPTER 16

UNDER THE LANCE

THE GREATER THE DISASTER, the slower the spread of information.

When people all across northern Africa and Eurasia transformed into pillars of salt, the full story disseminated slowly.

But once it did, all further attacks against the lance were suspended.

The weapon continued sailing the skies as if it owned them, and it kept growing in length.

"In a little more than six months," Hyuga noted, "the lance will catch up to its own tail and encircle the Earth."

The impossible kept occurring.

Shinji asked the question on everyone's minds. 《And what happens when it does?》

Shinji was in Cage Two. It was his turn to be on standby.

Hyuga held his palm at an angle and then turned it nearly vertical.

"One day, the Earth will buckle under the lance's strangulation."

In other words, total destruction. The world would no longer be able to sustain life.

《What kind of force is the lance using against us? Gravity?》

"I think it's something more than that."

With so many unanswered questions, Misato found herself surrounded by her staff on the command center's middle deck. She was doing her best to assuage their fears.

"Trois," Aoba said, "are you up for questions? I don't want you to overexert yourself."

"I am." Ayanami Rei Trois said. Her mental state had recovered enough for her to join the discussion, though she was still growing accustomed to being alone again.

"So, that black giant—" Aoba started to say, but Misato cut him off.

"Armaros."

"Right, Armaros. So, Armaros' scales must have been responsible for turning those mass-production Evas into zombified Angel Carriers...and for powering them, too, right?"

Toji tilted his head. "You mean...like batteries?"

"Armaros might have been using the scales to control the Carriers, too," Misato said, "not just power them. After all, one of them managed to—"

Asuka scowled. "Yeah, yeah, I let the lance's copy get stolen. But you're right, there seems to be some kind of organization."

Hyuga hummed in thought. "The scales might be portals capable of transmitting commands and power via quantum jumps."

"That's awfully convenient," Misato remarked.

"Quantum jumps occur within the Evas' bodies all the time," Hyuga said. "At least, that's our best explanation for how their nerve impulses travel so efficiently."

"And supposing the large plates we saw behind Armaros can extend that effect over vast distances..."

"The sigil seems to be part of how they function—a Quantum Resonance Signum."

"Q.R. Signum," Misato said.

Asuka folded her arms. "I'm more concerned about what that black giant—"

"Armaros!" the commander admonished.

"—what *Armaros* was saying. What the hell are we supposed to have failed, anyway?"

When the three Ayanamis had mentioned the Human Instrumentality Project, everyone present had frozen.

"Trois, was that what Armaros meant?" Asuka asked.

"What I felt in the gia—I mean, Armaros," Rei Trois said, correcting herself under Misato's glare. "Well, I don't really have words to describe it. I sensed a great pressure, like a wall."

"A wall?"

"A gear that can never stop turning," Trois explained. "Or like how plants and insects thrive throughout the year, but winter always comes to kill them."

"That sounds brutal."

"That pressure searched my mind for the words to say..."

The group let out a collective sigh.

"The Human Instrumentality Project," Toji said. "That was finished three years ago."

From Cage One, where she was fine-tuning Eva-02, Maya added, 《Finished in failure.》

"What was the Human Instrumentality Project?" Toji asked. "Did Dr. Akagi tell you anything about it?"

How many times have I been asked that? Maya thought.

《I don't know any more than anyone else.》 She sounded irritated. 《After the battle at HQ, Seele disappeared. We chased after them, scooping up every clue we could find. You've all seen that creepy CG movie, haven't you?》

The movie had been one of the few items left behind in Seele's facility.

Its purpose was unknown, but the consensus was that it had been made to present their plan.

"The one about how all people would abandon the boundaries that separate them, and we'd mix together in a red, soupy sea?" Toji asked.

The movie broke the process down into several steps. It was all nonsense, like a promotional video for some strange cult.

Taken alone, the movie might have been considered fiction, but its contents aligned with the information Kaji had uncovered—which had led Shinji to stop the Human Instrumentality Project.

"Sometimes I think the Instrumentality Project will be with us forever," Maya said.

The Human Instrumentality Project.

Seele, led by Kiel Lorenz, devised the plan and tasked Ikari Gendo and Fuyutsuki Kozo, among others, with carrying out the Project.

In the final stages of the Battle at Nerv HQ, the project was nearly realized, with Eva-02 as its central sacrifice.

The tree of life was etched into the heavens, the mass-production Evas danced in exaltation, and humanity glimpsed an apocalypse that defied their understanding.

But even afterward, people still believed that the project was the work of humans.

Was that really the case?

There had been the Giant of Light. And Adam. And Lilith.

Had Seele truly believed they could control such beings?

Or had they convinced themselves that the project was their creation?

The human race had defeated the Angels and avoided the dreaded Third Impact.

The Human Instrumentality Project was thwarted, and humanity gained a future.

Or so they thought.

But then Armaros had appeared, and its fragmented words, which had passed through Ayanami, sounded like a proclamation that the project would soon begin again.

Armaros appeared to be wiping the slate clean for a second attempt.

"Armaros sounded disdainful," Asuka said, "like a scientist cleaning up someone else's experiment."

The word, "experiment," felt accurate to Misato. She didn't like the implications.

"Does Armaros intend to clear everything from the table in order to start the next Human Instrumentality Project, like the great flood?" she asked. The idea sounded ludicrous. "After everything has been washed away, will new test subjects come sailing in on an ark?"

The ark represented a way for the few chosen survivors of the old world to escape into the new one.

When Armaros spoke through Ayanami, the personnel of Nerv Japan heard the voice. But the black giant also spoke by shaking the Earth. Here and there, people outside of Nerv heard the voice as well, and its message threw humankind into even greater turmoil.

Nerv

GOD'S IN HIS HEAVEN ALL'S RIGHT WITH THE WORLD

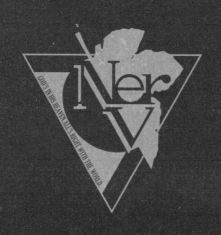

PART 4

NEON GENESIS

CLEARING THE STAGE

EVANGELION: ANIMA

NEON GENESIS
EVANGELION ANIMA

CHAPTER 17

PLANETARY TRANSFORMATION

SHINJI DREAMED.

His father used him like a tool, Asuka berated him, and Ayanami was off in her own apathetic world.

Shinji would have treasured even a pitying look from any one of them.

He constantly sought the approval of others—craving it, clinging to it—for proof that his existence had value.

He wanted to touch and be touched, but he also feared these things.

He was afraid of being told he was unneeded.

He put on his headphones, trying to drown his anxiety in the repeating music.

Tears welled in his eyes. *Why? Why is living this painful?*

《That is you in the next world.》

It was Kaworu's voice.

《You've performed too well in this world. You're going to be revised for the next cycle so that the Human Instrumentality Project will succeed.》

Revised...

《Do you know why they're so wary of Super Eva's heartbeat?》

Why?

《Because, by possessing a heart, Super Eva—and you with it—has become the most powerful entity in the world.》

Can it really be called a heart when no blood flows through it?

《Sure it can. A heartbeat is like a lantern atop a lighthouse or a torch held aloft. It says, "I'm here." A statement like that—an entity like you and Super Eva, firmly rooted in time and place—is nearly impossible to erase.》

I'm...having trouble following.

《Do your best. No matter what you are or what you become, I'm your ally.》

Whether part of the dream or the waking world, the ground rumbled far away.

The communications infrastructure was slowly crumbling.

To start, the geostationary satellites responsible for most broadcasts no longer sent or received signals. In fact, all satellites more than 20,000 kilometers above sea level were now unreachable—20,000 kilometers being the altitude of the Lance of Longinus's orbit.

When the decrease in Earth's gravitational pull caused a Russian satellite to deviate from its orbit, the satellite was observed striking some kind of barrier at that same altitude.

The lance hadn't simply claimed its orbit, it had completely isolated the Earth within a massive, invisible sphere, which scientists dubbed the Longinus Curtain.

A new picture emerged. Not only had the geostationary satellites deviated from their orbits, their signals had been cut off at the barrier. Observations of other astronomical objects also revealed slight distortions in the star map, further backing this theory.

The tectonic plates began moving on a larger scale. When the undersea cables started snapping, the communications shortage worsened.

In order to track of the changing geological state of the planet, an agreement was reached through the meager means of communication remaining. All operational particle accelerators would periodically fire neutrinos toward the Super-Kamiokande neutrino observatory in Gifu, Japan.

The angles of incidence and the times of arrival painted a picture of a rapidly shrinking Earth.

Postponing investigation into this constriction, the United States Air Force Orbital Combat Command attempted to destroy the Longinus Curtain but not the lance itself.

A squadron of military spacecraft, flying under the banner of the UN, launched twelve N_2 warheads at the Curtain. Not only was the attack entirely ineffective, but it also resulted in further harm to humanity. The explosions created a massive electromagnetic pulse, the majority of which didn't pass through the barrier but were neatly reflected by its smooth, concave inner surface. The energy converged on a city beneath the point of impact.

The city was annihilated.

NEON GENESIS
EVANGELION ANIMA

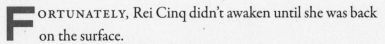

CHAPTER 18

FORTUNATELY, Rei Cinq didn't awaken until she was back on the surface.

In orbit, the diminutive Rei Six brought her Series-0.0 Eva alongside Cinq's, removed the slumbering Rei's entry plug, and brought her back to Earth, leaving Cinq's Eva in low orbit.

The order had been given to temporarily withdraw all Ayanamis from space.

When Cinq awakened, it quickly became clear that she had a personality distinct from Six's.

The three Ayanamis, now together on the Earth's surface, accompanied Maya to a UN question-and-answer session—more of an inquisition, really—regarding the Ayanamis' sluggish response to Armaros and the subsequent shooting of the lance. Commander Katsuragi Misato had just returned from a similar session. But the attack on the Lance of Longinus had been carried out at the UN's request, and historically, Misato bore all responsibility for the Ayanamis' actions. The UN wasn't supposed to circumvent the commander, and yet that's exactly what they were doing. Shinji found this breach of protocol unsettling.

Misato told him that the UN just needed a place to direct its anger. Nearly two million people had turned to salt, and the death toll from the subsequent disasters was at five figures and climbing.

"Europe was hit the hardest," Misato said, "and they probably want to find a scapegoat, but does anybody think about how *we* feel? *We're* the ones unable to show off all the strength we've built up."

She tried to pass the remark off as a joke, but she really did feel this way.

On the innermost rail of Nerv HQ's circular Grand Deck were three equidistant armored trains. Each held one end of a support cable suspending an observation module in the open space above the central shaft, beneath which the remnants of the old HQ had been sealed away inside the sarcophagus.

The observation module was supposed to be off limits, as were its support cables. But one day Shinji saw someone he recognized crossing the footbridge above one of the cables, and before he knew it, he was approaching her.

He cut across the rails and climbed onto the slowly moving armored train, wondering why he hadn't triggered any alarms. Standing at the inner edge, he hesitated, realizing how far the fall would be to the ground below.

Cautiously, he stepped out onto the cable and called to the person on the footbridge.

"Ayanami?"

The figure looked like Rei, but her hair color wasn't quite right, more silver than blue.

And why was she wearing a black knee-length dress in a place like this?

"You know we're not supposed to be here, right?" Shinji asked. "You *are* Ayanami...aren't you?"

"The Second Child—Asuka—said I was weird for not owning any formal clothes aside from my uniform. She helped me choose this dress." The figure turned and walked toward Shinji. "No, that's not right. The Second Child did all the choosing."

"Trois?"

Judging by her height, she had to be Trois. Cinq was a little bit taller.

But he thought that both of them had left HQ.

"The dress is Trois'. Everything in my room is hers."

Shinji stood on a small maintenance platform atop the slender support cable high in the air. The cable swayed slightly, making Shinji uneasy. He kept his hand firmly on the guardrail. The girl came close enough that he could feel the warmth of her body.

Her low-cut dress caught him off guard. She tilted her chin. Her clear eyes seemed to penetrate him.

"I intended to wear this for you," she said, "back when we were still one."

His bewilderment turned to shock. "You're...Ayanami Quatre."

The Ayanami who'd killed him. The Ayanami who'd escaped with her Series-0.0 Eva. Her mercury-colored hair swayed in the wind, and she gazed down at the sarcophagus as she spoke.

"Three years ago, why did you stop the Human Instrumentality Project? Don't you feel lonely? Don't you feel...unfulfilled?"

"It would be...strange to lose your self, don't you think?"

"That's why the me back then"—this Ayanami looked down at herself—"rejected Chief Ikari in the hope that *you* would be the one to fulfill me."

He found himself drawn to her drooping eyelashes. When she looked up at him, her hand was already behind his neck, drawing him closer.

"But you didn't!" she said.

Her heat poured into him.

Her lips, pressed against his, were warm.

When he'd kissed Asuka, it had been a stubborn, competitive, terrible kiss. Why had no one told him that kisses could be sweet?

The weight of her breath startled him. The world around faded.

"Wh-what are you doing?" Shinji stammered as he stepped back in surprise.

He felt as if he'd been swallowed by darkness. Panicking, he tried to stand firm, but his feet were no longer on the support cable.

He heard waves, faintly lapping against a shore.

I'm...at Lake Ashi? How?!

Shinji was standing on the eastern shore of Lake Ashi.

On the lake's surface bobbed a floating deck that had occasionally been used during weapons tests.

The view of Tokyo-3 and Nerv HQ on the northern shore was blocked by a cape, on Shinji's right, that extended into the lake and formed the base of Mount Komagatake to the east. The wind carried the faint sound of alarms ringing across the mountains.

What happened?

Shinji was still off-balance when Quatre let go of his hand.

She turned with an impish shrug and began walking along the shore. There was no one else in sight.

"It would be strange to lose your self?" she asked. "Is that the only reason? I think maybe you don't want other people to truly know you."

They came upon a dock that had fallen into neglect.

They passed between boats that had been hauled onto the beach and left there, their paint faded and chipped.

"Complete me, Ikari-kun."

The warmth from her lips lingered, and he was still shaken, but Shinji kept his wits about him.

"Do you know how the Human Instrumentality Project will end?" *Think, Shinji. Figure out what's going on!*

"I heard it will be wonderful."

"Did the voice tell you that?" Shinji meant the voice that had spoken through the Ayanamis' trance when Armaros appeared.

"You forced everyone else to come with you on this path. I'm not a complete person. The world is breaking. Can you at least take responsibility?"

If Shinji knew one thing, it was the answer to that question. "I can't. I value the time I spend with others. My self chose that over melting together."

Kaji, too, had once told him that this world was the product of his choice.

And Ayanami—Trois—said something similar to me recently.

Maybe I chose this world, but I can't carry that burden. Dealing with myself is the most I can do.

I'm always...

Shinji made a decision and started moving toward Quatre. This time, *he* would close the distance between them. Even if her mutant Eva was hidden nearby, as long as he captured her before she got inside it, he could fix this without a fight.

Quatre didn't move from where she stood on the dock, but behind her, three waterlogged boats, bobbing low on the lake's surface, suddenly shot into the sky.

"An A.T. Field!" Shinji gasped.

He threw himself to the side.

The boats crashed onto the weatherworn dock and re-bounded away.

Quatre was still facing Shinji. Behind her, the lake rose in a white swell.

A giant figure broke through the foam.

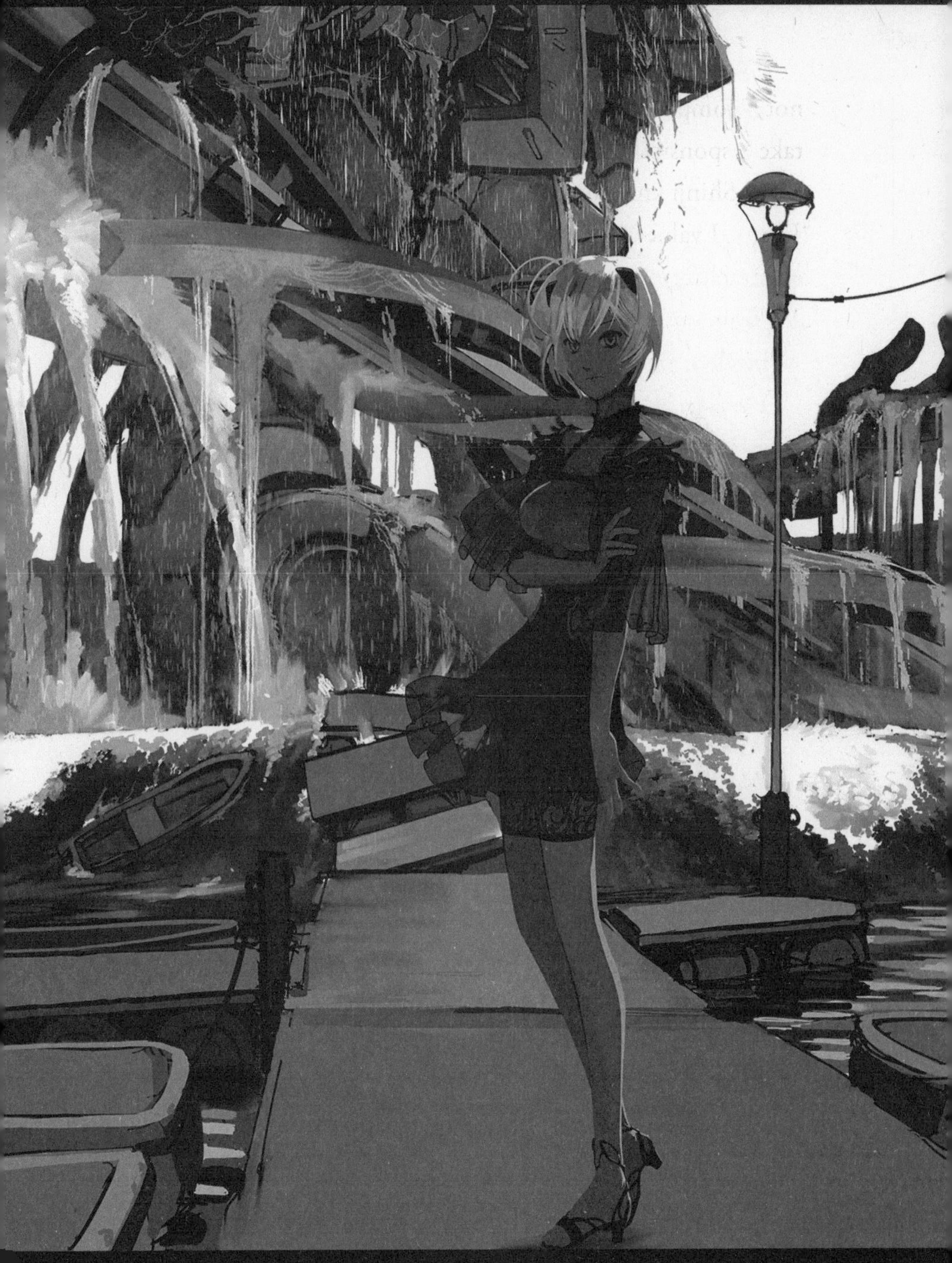

The mutant Eva-0.0 stood, water cascading off its body. "Damn it!"

The alarm had been triggered at Nerv HQ when a giant arm, seemingly belonging to a mutant Eva-0.0, reached up from the central shaft and grabbed two people from the observation module's support cables.

Inside Cage Two, Super Eva's visor opened as the Eva woke.

The cage crew immediately reported this to command.

Striding into the command center, Misato demanded, "Where's Shinji-kun?"

"According to his communicator, he's...on a support cable of the observation module?" Hyuga said. "Why would he be—"

"He's not," Aoba said, pulling up the feed from a nearby surveillance camera. He zoomed in on the support cable. "Not anymore, at least. He dropped his communicator."

"Is Super Eva going to go wild again?" Hyuga asked.

"The boy has been training hard every single day," Misato said. "Let's show a little faith in him. Open Cage Two's ceiling and raise the lift!"

As the mutant Eva-0.0 shook off a great mist of water, Ayanami Quatre looked toward HQ as if sensing something despite the mountain blocking their view.

"If I stop your heart," Quatre said, "maybe the Human Instrumentality Project can still be carried out. Our world won't have to end!"

Knowing this might be his last chance to capture Quatre, Shinji sprinted toward her, but the rising waves sent more boats flying toward him.

Shinji turned, running for his life. But as he dashed back onto the rocky shore, the waves swept him up. The water crashed, spraying mist, and then washed back, trying to pull him along with it. He clung tightly to the guardrail.

"Is that," he shouted, gasping for air, "what the voice told you?"

The mutant Eva scooped up Rei Quatre as she said, "No. I asked, but the voice didn't answer me."

Waves stirred, bubbles rising in the shape of a rectangle. Moments later, the gamma-ray laser cannon burst above the surface. The weapon had fused with the Eva's right arm.

Shinji cried out in surprise and scrambled under an over-turned boat.

With a flash of purple light, the mutant Eva fired its laser over the mountains at Super Eva, who had just come leaping over the ridge.

The laser surpassed its standard 1,900-gigawatt output and produced an EMP. The searing water heated Shinji's aluminum boat until it was bright red.

Shinji cried out in pain. He crawled out from under the boat, holding his left arm to his chest. Super Eva landed, and the ground shook. The Eva's left arm had been shot through, and it was badly injured. Nevertheless, the Eva shielded Shinji with its A.T. Field, gathered him up quickly in its good hand, and leaped away.

"The threat has been identified as Quatre's mutated Eva-0.0," Hyuga reported.

The command center had witnessed the Eva's emergence through a camera at the Mount Komagatake sniping post.

"She's appeared on our doorstep again!" Misato said.

A comms window opened, accompanied by a chime.

Shinji coughed. 《Hakone command, this is Ikari Shinji. I've entered Super Eva.》

"Shinji-kun!" Super Eva had somehow managed to reunite with Shinji. Misato felt a wave of relief, but this was no time to relax. "What's your situation?"

《I've encountered Quatre's Eva, and our left arm is badly injured.》

Misato glanced at the status board for the other Evas.

Hyuga noticed and said, "Unit Two is no good. Its internal cables are still being rerouted for the power source conversion."

"Why did this have to happen when the Reis are all here on Earth?"

Asuka's voice came over the line. 《I can attempt pre-entry in one of the Zero units. What do we have to lose?》

"Don't even think about it!" Misato barked. "The mental contamination could destroy you. The risk is too high."

The Evas had become more and more personalized. Currently, the only pilot substitutions that still worked—barely—were among the Ayanamis and the Zero-Series Evas. Now that the parallel clones' egos had awakened, even that had likely come to an end.

"Does Super Eva have any weapons?" Misato asked.

"A single prog knife," Hyuga answered.

"Activate the guided missiles in the city's defense sectors and the sniping post at Mount Komagatake."

"Yes, commander. But I'm not sure if they'll do the trick."

Misato knew they wouldn't, of course.

"Get ahold of the SSDF. Tell them that if the mutant Eva escapes the caldera, they're to use all means at their disposal. Whether that's maser howitzers or the Akashima, I don't care, so long as they kill it."

Standing in Lake Ashi, Super Eva wielded its single prog knife in close-quarters combat with the mutant.

Quatre's Eva raised its laser cannon, but at the last moment, Super Eva kicked the weapon up, and the beam scorched through the empty sky.

What if the city had been burned by that laser? Shinji thought. *I need to end this here.*

"Listen," he said. "Maya told me something. She said that you're confused because your sense of self is still maturing."

《Don't try to make that sound like a good thing. I can't hear my other selves. I'm alone now. I only hear one voice.》

Before Super Eva could bring its foot back down, the mutant spun, delivering a kick to its pivot leg, and Shinji went down.

But as his giant fell, Shinji glimpsed the mutant's exposed chest, and he saw something that wasn't supposed to be there—a black-red, glowing object piercing a joint in the armor plating.

"Hakone command! One of those black-red scales is in the mutant's chest. A Q.R. Signum!"

How had Quatre's Eva been altered so drastically? How had it suddenly appeared in one place, only to vanish without a trace as the Angel Carriers had?

"Quatre... Your identity..."

Did Armaros force her ego to manifest?

《The first thing I knew was terror. Terror from the pain being driven into my chest. Terror at the thought of being ripped away from myself, being made to be alone!》

How terrible...

Shinji finally understood what had happened to the Ayanamis.

Quatre was the vector for Armaros' impulses.

Shinji kept the prog knife hidden until the last possible

moment. He slashed the blade up from beneath the lake's surface and straight into the Q.R. Signum in the mutant Eva's chest.

Clang!

A strong field—possibly generated by the scale itself—protected the Signum.

"Quatre!" Shinji shouted. "Get rid of that scale. It's making you act crazy."

The prog knife's tip was frozen in place, a hair's breadth away from the Q.R. Signum. The blade glowed red with heat.

《This scale gives me incredible power. Resistance is meaningless, and it removes all meaning, anyway.》

"You mean because of the voice? If you let that thing manipulate you..."

Failing to penetrate the field, the prog knife flew out of Super Eva's grasp.

The mutant Eva swung its laser cannon. This time Shinji grabbed the Eva's legs, and the two giants staggered onto the eastern shore.

《Shinji!》 It was Misato. 《We can't allow that mutated Eva to escape again. Subdue it by any means necessary. We'll accept all outcomes. Understood?》

Shinji understood. She meant dead or alive.

Shinji recalled when an Angel had taken control of Eva-03 with Toji inside, and Shinji had received a similar order to subdue.

Super Eva's heart fluttered.

"Understood," he replied, but he refused to accept the order. His mind raced to think of an alternative.

Quatre spoke. 《If you weren't alive, the Human Instrumentality Project would have succeeded, and this world would have avoided calamity!》

Is that true?

《If you weren't alive, I wouldn't have had to know fear and loneliness!》

Really?

"If you want to kill me again—"

At the corner of his vision, Shinji saw three next-gen SSDF maser howitzers driving along the highway outside the caldera. But something wasn't right.

Why weren't their ID icons layered onto my display?

The command center was hiding information from him.

Misato must have realized that when the moment came, he wouldn't be able to kill Quatre.

The mutant Eva had broken free, but he grabbed the giant by the shoulders. Then, making sure the SSDF's howitzers could see, he kicked Quatre's Eva, knocking it down.

"If you want to kill me again," Shinji repeated, "why did you wear that dress for me? Somewhere in there, you're still the Ayanami I knew, aren't you?"

He brought his foot down with all his strength.

But the strike glanced off Quatre's Eva and hit the ground.

When the cloud of sediment cleared, the mutant Eva was gone. Shinji had let Quatre—his killer—escape.

"**T**HAT ONE was rather big," Maya said.

There had been another earthquake.

The Eurasian tectonic plate was contracting toward its center, and an offshoot of the North American plate had been dragged along until it finally snapped in two.

The plate containing the Kamchatka Peninsula broke along a line extending from the Commander Islands in the east to the Russian city of Magadan in the west. It was the birth of a smaller, independent plate that included eastern Japan, though some time passed before any geologists realized what had happened. When the cause of the great earthquake was discovered, this new plate would be named after the Sea of Okhotsk.

In Cage One, behind Eva-00 and the grounded Eva-0.0, Eva-02 was being modified for a lunar expedition. When the earthquake subsided, work resumed.

"Paint it the color of the moon, please," Asuka said.

The young woman had gone through many changes lately, but her rejection of her signature red color still came as a surprise.

Six's Eva-0.0 was reassigned to Cinq, who would accompany Asuka and Eva-02 on a lunar sortie. Armaros hadn't been seen since throwing the Lance of Longinus at the Earth.

If the Angel Carriers were any indication, Armaros was likely capable of appearing and disappearing anywhere at will. But with no other leads, the search would begin at the place their enemy had last appeared.

The plan was being pushed by the European members of the UN Security Council, who had suffered terrible losses, but

Asuka nevertheless agreed that this scouting mission was the right choice.

In the old days of space exploration, astronauts had planted several laser retroreflector arrays on the moon's surface. To better understand the Longinus Curtain, observers on Earth fired lasers of different spectra at the reflectors and measured the time the light took to travel.

This data, combined with the distortion in the star map, suggested that the Curtain was a kind of gap in space.

In other words, like an A.T. Field, the barrier created a phase contrast.

The effect of the USAF Orbital Combat Command's N_2 bombs lent further credence to this theory.

The idea behind N_2 bombs and reactors was to recreate the Angels' S^2 Engines with human technology back when the Angels' existence could only be speculated.

But at first, the technology wasn't controllable. The only success the engineers had found was to redirect the energy into an explosive weapon that rivaled the power of a nuclear warhead. The product was the N_2 bomb.

When multiple bombs had exploded against the Longinus Curtain, the resulting energy was unable to cross the phase contrast and instead manifested as shock waves.

The engineers hadn't been able to punch a hole through the barrier, but they had caused it to shake.

The new plan was to use an A.T. Field to negate the phase contrast, which meant sending an Eva piloted by a human. Under different circumstances, support might have been available from an orbital Eva-0.0, but this time, there would be no reinforcements.

"I have to take this seriously," Asuka said.

This time, she fully recognized that stubbornness alone wouldn't get her there and back again.

The modified Eva-02 Allegorica, a.k.a. the Unlimited Flight Type Reconnaissance-in-Force Spec Eva Unit-02 UX-1 Allegorica, had been so named because the unit looked like it could have come out of a fantastical allegory.

For one thing, the Allegorica had two rear legs and a body like a centaur. The added bulk would help the Eva remain stable during the long-distance flight.

Second, two large wings provided Eva-02, for the first time, with the ability to fly.

An N_2 reactor generated gravitons to power the Eva. Even the most cutting-edge technology could only manage to produce miniscule artificial tidal fields, but with the Allegorica, hundreds of tidal fields worked in parallel within artificial-diamond slits to create a considerably more powerful effect.

Getting the UN to approve the development of this technology for the Eva had been a hard sell, but when the graviton thrusters were tested on old Russian fighter planes, the results had been better than anticipated. They were so good, in fact, that the test aircraft were sent to Hakone for use in real combat.

Additional N_2 thrusters had been placed at the end of each wing to provide propulsion, but with skillful manipulation of the gravitational tilt, the long trip to the moon could be achieved without expending any propellant.

Two-phase contrast power generators protruded even farther out from the wingtips. By extending beyond the Eva's A.T. Field, these generators could draw power from the phase differential between the space inside the field and out, like a kind of regenerative energy system.

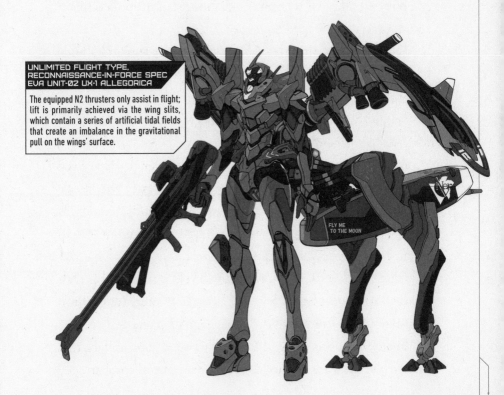

UNLIMITED FLIGHT TYPE,
RECONNAISSANCE-IN-FORCE SPEC
EVA UNIT-02 UX-1 ALLEGORICA

The equipped N2 thrusters only assist in flight; lift is primarily achieved via the wing slits, which contain a series of artificial tidal fields that create an imbalance in the gravitational pull on the wings' surface.

FLY ME
TO THE MOON

Of all the child pilots, Asuka possessed the highest synchronization rate with her Eva and was far and away the most adept at field generation.

Shinji and his Super Eva were tremendously powerful, but they were still relatively unstable, to the point where no one knew what might happen with them next. For that reason, they hadn't been chosen to undertake this extended mission.

Asuka had always regarded Eva-02 as a mere tool to help her achieve success.

She still believed that the Eva had stolen her mother, or her mother's soul, from her.

For that, she hated the thing, and she had never hesitated to push it to the point of destruction if it helped her achieve her own goals.

But during the Battle at Nerv HQ, she felt like she'd seen her mother inside Eva-02.

And now there was Super Eva.

Shinji said that his mother had disappeared from inside Eva-01.

Would the presence Asuka sensed in Eva-02 disappear as well?

After the battle at Nerv, she did everything differently.

Her synchronization rate with Eva-02 became more stable than that of any other pilot.

She became less likely to rely solely on force, and it stopped being such a struggle to raise her success rates.

Asuka was a realist. She didn't actually believe that Eva-02 was her real mother.

But this time, she'd decided to embark on the mission with Eva-02 Allegorica and that they would return together.

Asuka strode down the catwalk, her heels clicking loudly as she barked, "Hey, what are you painting that gold for?"

"It's an electromagnetic-resistant surface," a put-upon crewman replied. "Like I said, I'll paint over it however you want, but *later.*"

NEON GENESIS
EVANGELION ANIMA

ARMAROS HAD SAID that Super Eva's heartbeat must not be written onto the parchment of time.

"You're all going to school," Misato said.

"What?" the seventeen-year-olds protested in unison. *During this state of emergency?*

"Just as Super Eva's heart keeps a steady pulse, we must continue our daily rhythms. We will live our lives with intent and purpose and not fall into chaos."

Misato didn't believe that everything in Armaros' message and Shinji's dream was true.

But the fact remained that the enemy was bringing devastation on a catastrophic scale.

What Misato feared most was that humanity, confronted with this overwhelming power, might give up and abandon all resistance.

It didn't help that this new enemy wielded words as its weapon. Misato suspected that the religious allusions in Armaros' messages would give them more power over people than they might otherwise.

She didn't want the children, who would be needed in the fight, or the civilians to give up.

Therefore, she would make sure they maintained some sense of normalcy. If the worst should happen, the trivial and mundane might become their last treasure.

After classes had ended for the day, Shinji emerged from the school's entrance hall.

"I can't believe how exhausted I am," he muttered.

Shinji understood Misato's logic, but an unknown enemy had declared war on all of humanity. It was all well and good for Misato to tell him to resume his school routine, but Shinji couldn't switch his emotional state that easily.

"Ikariii," a lilting voice with a childish lisp called out.

"Yeah?" Shinji turned to see Rei Six spilling out of the entryway. Because she was so short, the school uniform, an above-the-knee dress, looked more like a full-length skirt.

Six was the other source of Shinji's exhaustion.

As for why she was attending high school, the girl had insisted that no matter the age of her physical body, on the inside, she was the same age as the other Ayanamis, and Misato acquiesced.

Today was Six's first day of school after gaining independence from the other Ayanamis, and she'd been hyped up all day long, acting on every impulse.

Shinji wondered if she really had inherited all of Trois' knowledge. Six couldn't seem to sit still for a moment. Even the cutesy way she ran toward him now filled him with dread.

Six leaped at him.

Their faces crashed together, and Shinji saw stars. The pair tumbled to the ground outside the school entrance.

"Owwww," they said in unison. They'd both fallen on their bottoms, huddled together, holding their faces in their hands. The other students on their way out of the school stopped to stare.

The two groaned in pain.

Then Six kissed Shinji.

Flustered, he quickly pushed her away, sputtering. "Wh-wh... Huh?"

"The Quatre-me felt a thrill from that, no matter how she denied it. But the Six-me doesn't." Six pressed her finger here and there on her lips with a dissatisfied expression. "Why is that?"

"Wh-why? How should I know?"

Actually, he did know, or at least...he had a good idea. According to Maya, Six's body couldn't keep pace with her knowledge.

Shinji's mind swam with the sexual development vocabulary he'd had to study in his junior-high health class, but he wasn't about to explain the awkward subject to Six. Doing so would only cause more trouble.

Wait... What did she say about Quatre?

"What happened?" Toji said, emerging from the school among a group of students in track jackets.

The crowd parted to form a path for Asuka and Rei Cinq.

Trois arrived a little later, having stopped by the student council meeting room first.

The group had decided beforehand that they would leave school together to make less work for the security team's secret service agents, who were doubtlessly hovering nearby and keeping track of the pilots during the heightened state of alert.

At school, some students had made jokes—if they could be called that—about how there were so many empty desks that a few more Ayanamis wouldn't be a problem. Even this tightly supervised city had seen deaths from recent events.

Shuffling personnel from posting to posting only accomplished so much, and the effects extended to the school.

Overhead, the Lance of Longinus traced a thin white line—a little longer every day—across the sky.

"You can't act like that, Six," Ayanami Cinq said. "You're embarrassing Ikari-kun."

The child pilots, present and former, merged with the crowd of normal students and began their walk.

"Ah," Asuka said, "now *this* is a day to remember. A first-year asked Cinq out in the hallway."

"What?" Shinji and Toji interrupted in unison.

Asuka sighed and scrunched her eyebrows together. "That isn't the surprise, boys. Get this—Cinq let him down kindly and gently."

"She did what?" Toji asked.

All eyes went to Cinq.

"Well," she said, "I would've felt bad for him if I didn't give him a straight answer."

Cinq smiled. She'd spent more time growing in the artificial womb, and her body had matured a bit—further than Trois or Quatre. Standing with the group, she appeared to be a year ahead of them.

"Hmm," Toji said. "That doesn't sound very Ayanami-ish. That's weird, Cinq."

"I just don't want to get too close to anyone," Cinq said. "Because they'll learn..."

"Learn what?" Toji asked.

She didn't answer. Given how Six had manifested Rei's deep-seated innocence, then which part of Ayanami's psyche had awakened Cinq's individuality?

The minds of each Ayanami had begun walking disparate, less "Ayanami-ish" paths.

Ikari Gendo, the former Nerv commander, had created parallel clones of Ayanami in great numbers, though her soul could only attach to one at a time.

But now there were three new Ayanamis.

That Armaros had provided the impetus for their awakening didn't sit well with Trois.

Cinq and Six now exhibited their own distinct personalities, and Trois was feeling alone.

She trudged along at the rear of the group. The other two were gradually revealing aspects of herself that would otherwise have remained hidden, but Trois didn't have the self-awareness to recognize it. Instead, she just felt more and more out of place.

Even with the additional Ayanamis, the old circle of friends still felt they were lacking something. Hikari and Kensuke were absent. Kensuke had realized that he would never become a pilot. He'd joined Nerv's security intelligence department, and they'd hardly seen him since.

"Where's the class rep today?" Shinji asked.

"*You're* the class rep," Toji replied.

"How long is your head going to be stuck in junior high?" Asuka asked. "Where is Hikari, anyway? I haven't heard from her. Do you know, Suzuhara?"

"She's in Australia. I got an e-mail from her saying she's stuck there due to the tectonic instability. I guess she's safe. She was smiling in the picture she sent. I was kinda surprised, because I'd heard she was vacationing with her family."

"Well, as long as she wasn't in Europe," Asuka said.

Asuka didn't know that Hikari had indeed been caught in the catastrophe the lance had wrought upon Europe. These days, conversations inevitably drifted toward current events.

"It feels like every country is in a race," Toji said.

"They all want to be the one that finds the ark," Shinji replied.

"Well, the Earth might be doomed," Toji said, "and it doesn't look like we're escaping through the Longinus Curtain."

"But Armaros mentioned an ark," Shinji said.

"That's right, the ark," Trois said.

"I wonder if that's our way to escape," Asuka pondered.

"Everyone seems to believe it is," Shinji replied. "But that's assuming that Armaros' idea of an ark is the same as ours."

"I want ice cream," Six added.

"For some reason, it feels credible," Cinq said.

"It's ridiculous," Asuka said. "Every country is sending disaster relief teams to every other country, but they're all just snooping around for the ark. It's obvious because *every* country is getting hit by the disaster, and yet they're still sending out teams. How else do you explain it?"

"Have you considered that they could be acting out of compassion and putting the misfortunes of others ahead of their own?" Shinji asked.

"It's possible," Asuka replied, "but there *are* organizations going around trying to dig things up."

"I hear Kensuke and Kaji-san are having trouble with that in Cyprus right now," Toji said. "Special forces are all over the place."

Shinji stopped in his tracks. "Hold on. That's got to be classified information. How do you know about it, Toji?"

Toji kept walking, casually waving a hand. "With the personnel change tomorrow, I'll be the acting deputy commander."

"What?!" said Shinji, Asuka, and Six in unison.

"Now, I'm not looking for any congratulations, but... Soryu! I'd appreciate it if you didn't look like this means we're all doomed. And you, Ayanamis, could one or two of you try offering me something other than pity? I thought you were supposed to have different personalities."

"It's big news," Trois said.

"Well, I can't help it! I didn't want it either, but the higher you go, the more chronically understaffed they are, right? Like at the UN Security Council's inquest..." Toji scowled at the smallest Ayanami. "By the way, you really put your foot in it big time, Six. I don't think Maya-san was able to cover for you, either."

"What did she say?" Shinji asked.

"That Quatre kissed Shinji," Six said.

"What?!" Asuka shouted.

Shinji suddenly found himself in a minefield.

She mentioned that earlier, he thought, finally putting the pieces together. *The Ayanamis have been saying that their mental link with Quatre was severed, but what if that's not true?*

Toji explained that Six had accidentally revealed to the UN that Shinji had let Ayanami Quatre—an enemy whose Eva could operate without restrictions—escape.

Blood rushed to Shinji's head, and he suddenly felt dizzy. "Let's get ice cream," he said weakly.

Shinji began walking toward a small store. Six followed after him, and then the rest of the group.

"Hold on, Shinji," Asuka said. "Explain yourself!"

"Why are you getting upset, Asuka?" Toji asked. "She's a little girl. It was just a kiss."

"Wait, are you talking about *Six?*"

Toji quickly changed the subject. "Anyway, everyone's gotten so specialized lately—including all of you—that the organization doesn't work smoothly."

"Oh, is that so?" Asuka said. "So, that's why they picked you, because you're not special at anything?"

Toji would soon learn, upon taking up his new position, that Nerv Japan—including the security intelligence department—had completely lost track of Hikari and her family.

"Toji," Six whined, "I can't reach!"

She was hopping up and down in front of the ice cream freezer outside the store.

The wind carried the chime from a nearby elementary school announcing the end of the school day. The melody was familiar, Dvořák's Symphony No. 9, "From the New World."

"All right, all right," Toji said.

He lifted Six so she could reach through the freezer's top door.

Just then, a flock of doves took flight from the roofs of the buildings lining the street.

Behind the doves—as if chasing them away—the sound of flapping wings came from over the caldera's outer mountains.

"What is that?" Toji asked. "Whoa!"

In his surprise, he dropped Six into the freezer, and she let out a startled protest.

An enormous swarm of birds soared overhead like a black cloud.

The group looked up.

Shinji, Asuka, and Ayanamis Trois and Cinq watched the torrent of birds pass.

The swarm flew south, past Lake Ashi and over Mount Daikanzan. When they disappeared, silence fell.

A few days later, humanity would realize that every bird had disappeared from the face of the Earth.

CHAPTER 21

▷ ── **THE PEGASUS TAKES FLIGHT**

ON AN UNMANNED, offshore launch platform near Tanegashima, Ayanami Cinq blasted back into space in the Series-0.0 Eva.

Meanwhile, in Hakone, Eva-02's graviton thrusters filled the caldera with an unpleasant, dissonant noise.

Asuka's Allegorica gently rose from the floating deck-turned-launch pad on Lake Ashi.

Once the tidal field cascade had generated sufficient lift, Asuka let go of the launch pad, and her Eva shot into the sky.

From Asuka's point of view, she felt like the Earth had turned upside down and thrown her away. It didn't feel good.

Asuka wasn't supposed to switch on the assist rockets until after she'd reached the aerodynamic ceiling, but a gust of wind threatened to blow her into a nearby mountain, and she fired her thrusters for a few seconds to avoid it.

Her communications display opened, and Toji spoke to her from the command center.

《Hello? Can you hear me? Asuka, is everything all right?》

"Don't bother me! Listen, you guys had better protect the Earth while we're gone."

She felt a twinge of sadness at leaving and immediately regretted saying anything.

《Okay, until you reach an altitude of 190 kilometers, you're— *pffff*—bwa ha ha ha ha! Six, what happened to your hair?!》

"Wait, what?"

Through the hydrospeaker, Asuka heard several voices burst into laughter.

《Have you gone punk rock?》 Misato asked.

《Six, where have you been?》 That was Shinji.

A single technician attempted to stay focused. 《At the takeoff stage, static electricity built up on the gravitons, and—》

Toji's laugher drowned her out. 《Oh, that is *too good!* You look like you stuck a fork in a socket!》

Then Shinji. 《Quit laughing so hard, Toji, you're going to make me lose it, too—aha ha ha ha!》

《That's it.》 Misato's voice. 《I need to get a picture of this. Let's get the 02-Allegorica on the screen in the background.》

"Even Misato's in on it," Asuka grumbled to herself. "C'mon, guys, take this seriously."

But it was this kind of levity that Asuka was flying to the moon to protect.

NEON GENESIS
EVANGELION ANIMA

CHAPTER 22

THE LAST DOVE

M ISATO LISTENED as Maya reported what had transpired
at the UN inquisition.

The Ayanamis were aware of the kiss Quatre and Shinji had
shared.

The mental link between Trois, Quatre, Cinq, and Six
remained severed, either because their individual identities had
manifested or because of Armaros' scale—the Q.R. Signum.

But they could still connect, albeit unexpectedly. When
Quatre's emotions had heightened on the edge of Lake Ashi, the
other Ayanamis had heard her voice—and they were aware when
Shinji had purposefully failed to capture her.

Seated before the panel of UN questioners, Six let slip what
Shinji had done.

Every nation of the world had been plunged into potential
tectonic catastrophe, but the strongest rebukes came from the
countries of Europe—who'd already lost 1.9 million souls to the
lance's light.

Was Nerv Japan, they asked, truly fit to be entrusted with Evangelions?

Was Nerv Japan wielding humanity's most powerful weapons at the whims of individual pilots?

Misato gave Shinji a thorough dressing-down.

The fact that she was lecturing the most powerful human on Earth was not lost on either of them, but it was precisely his power that made this necessary.

Shinji understood, and he took his licks.

This willingness proved that—at least for now—Shinji was still human. But if faced with the same situation in the future, would he be able to take Quatre down?

He was no closer to knowing the answer.

The UN dispatched a military attaché to assist Misato in the command center as a tactical advisor—and, in truth, a watchdog.

"Have you considered a punishment?" the man asked, jumping right into his job.

Misato frowned. "What, like tossing him into detention?"

"Certainly not."

The supposed advisor said that UNTRP forces had been performing training exercises in Siberia when the Okhotsk Plate split off, and they had proceeded to provide disaster relief on the Kamchatka Peninsula and then northern Hokkaido.

A JSSDF training base located between the cities of Sapporo and Chitose had been repurposed as a staging ground for aid moving in and out of the country. The advisor suggested that Misato send Super Eva there to assist as its operating range was essentially limitless.

The suggestion was more straightforward than the commander had expected.

"His security is still a concern," Misato said. "If I send him there, it would only be for two days. Three at most."

"It could be—how do you say it in Japanese—the *Kaomise?* Like a stage debut at the beginning of a new production season. It would be good for the people to recognize that Evas aren't our enemies."

After what felt like an eternity, Shinji returned to his private quarters inside HQ. He stepped through the doorway with a heavy sigh, and then, head reeling from being yelled at, he surveyed the room.

"Hm? Why is that on?"

The LCD wall was supposed to switch off automatically when the room was empty. Instead, the screen displayed a vast blue sky. Meanwhile, the lights were supposed to turn on when he entered, but they hadn't, and the room's AI, which usually reported his missed messages and other useful information, remained silent.

"Is it broken?" Shinji asked himself. "Wait... What's that?!"

In the center of the room stood a small cage with a white dove inside.

Wham!

Possibly startled by Shinji, the bird became agitated and began slamming itself into the bars of the cage.

Wham! Wham!

Unable to bear watching the poor creature hurt itself, Shinji lifted the cage with one hand and opened its door with the other.

The dove flew straight at the wall, and—

Shinji gasped. The bird didn't strike the wall but rather flew into the blue sky of the LCD and off into the distance.

Shinji heard Kaworu's voice.

《That was the last dove. It was supposed to be your pilot, to take you to the next world.》

When Shinji reached his hand out to the blue sky, the image disappeared. The display was off and cool to the touch.

He suddenly noticed the noise of his air conditioner. The room's AI began speaking.

"Your schedule is clear for the rest of the day. There have been no messages, deliveries, or visitors."

The ceiling light switched on, and Shinji looked down at his hand. The birdcage was gone.

THE CURTAIN

RATHER THAN FLY directly to the moon, Cinq's Eva-0.0 and Asuka's Eva-02 increased their orbit gradually. The plan was to make contact with the Longinus Curtain at the shallowest possible angle.

Asuka looked at the Earth overhead.

She'd read a report stating that the shifting tectonic plates had caused the Arabian Peninsula to begin rotating counterclockwise.

The Himalayas had risen sharply, and the Indian subcontinent had begun sinking under the Eurasian plate to its north. The people there had begun fleeing to the surrounding countries, but the landmass, with one of the highest populations in the world, was moving faster than the people who inhabited it.

The tectonic plates were comparatively light and didn't typically sink, aside from a few specific locations.

When they did sink, it meant the mantle beneath them was shrinking on a massive scale.

By measuring the inside of the Earth, geologists theorized

that the Earth was losing material from its inner layers. Both the expansive mantle and the core were gradually vanishing.

"It's hard to believe," Asuka said to herself, "that the Earth is losing weight and the plates are butting into each other."

Wait...

If the Lance of Longinus is using some strange power to shrink the Earth, then where is all that missing material going?

《Unit Two—Soryu-san.》Cinq's voice crackled through the hydrospeaker. 《We're 600,000 milliseconds from making contact with the barrier.》

Asuka gazed into the void.

She called me Soryu-san.

The primary Ayanami, Rei Trois, had called Asuka "the Second Child" at first. It had taken two years before she started calling her "Asuka."

And now that Cinq has formed her individual identity, she calls me Soryu-san.

Cinq was making more of an effort to be sociable than the other Ayanamis, but Asuka had trouble figuring out who the real Cinq was. She was easy to talk to, but sometimes Asuka got the sense that the girl was only going through the motions. It was hard to tell if she truly meant the things she said.

I don't know... She might be a good person, but if she isn't genuine, then who's going to take the first step and be her friend?

Maybe I should mind my own business.

Asuka spoke into to her cockpit's computer. "Connect to Earth. Nerv Japan, Hakone command center."

The display read, TRANSMISSION ANTENNA ORIENTATION NORMAL. LOCKING ON TO LOW ORBITAL NETWORK. SYSTEMS IN ORDER.

So then, some satellites are still managing to hold on to their fuel.

"Command center, this is Unit Two. We're ten minutes from the Curtain, and I'm seeing irregularity in the distribution of the Van Allen radiation belts' magnetic flux density. I think the Lance of Longinus is stirring up Earth's magnetic field, but whatever the cause, the simulated measurements from thirty minutes ago are way off."

《Hakone command to Unit Two Allegorica. Please proceed.》

"When I align the gravitons on my wings, they're picking up vibrations in the gravity waves coming from the Longinus Curtain. I think the lance is causing the barrier to vibrate."

Another voice came over the line.

《Asuka.》

"Yes, Shinji, you don't need to say it. I'm going to get this done." Asuka spoke without the bravado the old her would have used. "Watch me."

《Unit Two, this is Unit Cinq. We're 200,000 milliseconds from the Curtain.》

"I'm filling my plug with LCL to prepare for the impact."

All the measurements indicated that the Longinus Curtain was, as suspected, a phase-shifted space. If that was indeed the case, then an A.T. Field with the same phase differential should be able to open a way through.

At first glance, there seemed to be nothing ahead, but as Asuka neared the barrier, she began to see a faint, rainbow-colored light—the Longinus Curtain. The barrier's thickness, if it had any, was as close to zero as possible, and yet the field distorted Earth's view of everything in outer space.

"Counting down to contact. T-minus 7, 5, 3. Unit Two, mark."

《Unit Cinq, mark.》

When the two Evas manifested their A.T. Fields and connected with the barrier, a tremendous force immediately pushed back against them and altered their course.

The A.T. Fields made contact with the Longinus Curtain, and interference patterns bursting with color spread outward.

The fields rumbled and shook. Maybe the barrier wasn't as smooth as it looked.

The spherical Curtain itself rotated around the Earth, and Eva-02 Allegorica and Eva-0.0 maintained a slightly faster orbital velocity, with a slightly larger radius. As a result, they slid along the interior surface of the Curtain.

But that wasn't the only reason the barrier hadn't repelled them.

"It's pulling us in," Asuka said.

Whatever the force was, it wasn't gravity.

This force was preventing them from using their A.T. Fields

to extricate themselves from the barrier. But aside from the vibrations, the friction was nearly nil, and they were free to move in two dimensions along the inner surface of the sphere.

"Cinq, can you still control your Eva?"

《Only as much as you. I don't think we could escape if we needed to abandon the mission.》

"Then all we can do is push forward."

Following the plan, Asuka attempted to punch a hole through the area of contact between the Curtain and her A.T. Field. The tip of her prog knife created a tiny opening that scattered brilliant light.

Ripples, like the wake of a ship, formed on the barrier.

"I'm going to make this quick!"

She focused on the blade. As she wrenched the breach open, countless phase-differential pockets spilled out, radiating different wavelengths before evaporating into nothing.

As the knife slid along the barrier, the opening became an ever widening ellipse.

Just then, a voice, staticky from the interference, came over her hydrospeaker.

《Urgent message from Hako—Command. The lance has cha—course!》

Asuka clicked her tongue. "We've been noticed."

That possibility had been factored into their strategy, and they'd timed their contact with the Curtain so that the Lance of Longinus was at the point in its orbit farthest away from them. But would that buy Asuka enough time?

"This is—ne Command. The lance made a ninety-degree turn along the Curtain and is maintaining speed at ninety kilometers per second. That's—shortest—"

The lance veered toward them on the shortest course, without losing any speed. It was better than if it had left the barrier and flown toward them in a straight line, but among the expected outcomes, this was the worst.

Why does everything always have to go like this? Haven't you heard of the laws of physics?!

The hole in the barrier had grown, but it was still small—too small for an Eva to pass through. Asuka and Cinq had no way to remove themselves from the barrier and drop their orbit, and they didn't have enough time to figure out an alternative.

The lance would intercept them in another 600,000 milliseconds.

More than enough time to widen the—

But Asuka's thoughts were interrupted when the Curtain shook. Her Eva-02 Allegorica and Cinq's Eva-0.0 lurched violently, sliding up the surface of the barrier.

The hole became distant and then suddenly closed.

"Scheisse!" Asuka said.

《This is—kone—mand to Ev—Two. What happened? Your orbi—vector changed.》

《The Curtain shook without warning!》 Cinq said.

The two Evas slid a long distance across the barrier before finally stabilizing again.

Asuka was going to have to start over.

"What was that?"

《I'm not sure.》 Cinq's voice was shaky. 《But I think the whole Curtain might have shifted due to the lance changing course.》

"You've got to be kidding. That wasn't in the briefing!"

They'd already lost too much of the time they had until the lance arrived. They needed a new plan.

"Cinq, I'm going to alter my orbit. Synchronize your navigation system with mine."

《Synchronized. Now what?》

"We'll shift our orbit so that we're travelling away from the lance, and I'll work quickly. We'll buy as much time as we can before it catches up."

《But we'll be forty degrees inclined from the moon's plane of rotation!》

"We can worry about that after we're on the other side."

For the second attempt, Asuka and Cinq didn't remain stationary relative to the barrier. Instead, they traveled faster to take advantage of centrifugal inertia and help the prog knife cut through.

They had originally intended to use this method to evade the Lance of Longinus, should the weapon catch up with them, but now that they knew it could change course without losing velocity, evading it was no longer an option.

Even if they dodged out of the lance's path at the last second, it would simply turn and keep coming.

"We could separate—" Cinq began, but she cut herself off.

She'd come up with the idea to split the two Evas up along the surface of the barrier. That way, one of them would have more time.

But she realized that if they separated, they'd each only have one A.T. Field to cut through the Curtain. The slower cutting would cancel out any time they gained.

"Unit Two," Cinq said, "I'm going to boost my S^2 Engine to emergency output levels."

"Do it," Asuka said. She returned her focus to the virtual display, where her prog knife was digging into the barrier.

Eva-0.0 placed its left hand behind Eva-02's shoulder and fired backward with its Field Stepping Booster. Cinq focused her

A.T. Field onto the tip of the massive gamma-ray laser cannon in her Eva's other hand and worked at widening the small hole Asuka had opened.

《Switching now.》 Cinq's S² Engine's output increased sharply, and Asuka could feel it rumbling on her back. Propelled by the full force of Eva-0.0's FSB, Eva-02's prog knife pressed deeper into the barrier.

Through the Eva's feedback link, Asuka could feel a tremendous weight on her arm. She wasn't sure which would buckle first, the Curtain or her Eva. Amid the roar of the vibrations, Asuka heard Eva-02's chest creak.

Asuka grunted under her breath. She refused to back down.

The tip of Eva-0.0's laser cannon passed through the hole Asuka was struggling to open, and Cinq manifested her A.T. Field around the cannon's barrel.

"We can do this!" Asuka said.

But in that moment, she knew something was amiss. The S² Engine's output was increasing without stopping.

Nothing in the Series-0.0 Eva could have caused this. Was this the barrier at work?

No S² Engine had ever been successfully recovered until Shinji's Eva-01 had ingested one of the Angel Zeruel's. Whenever an Angel's S² Engine was destroyed, the Angel died in a gigantic explosion; and whenever an Angel was killed with its engine intact, the engine rapidly decayed.

When Nerv's engineers had attempted to salvage the S² Engines from the mass-production Evas, they'd placed the Evas' corpses on artificial life support to trick the engines into perceiving that their hosts were still alive. Even then, the engineers had had to remove the engines with their spines intact and reinstall them externally on the receiving Evas.

Should we jettison the engine?

If they did, Cinq's Eva would run out of power in minutes. She would never reach the moon, and even the trip home would be a gamble.

But Asuka knew of one last-ditch method to get Cinq out—abandon the Eva at the barrier and escape with the entry plug's thruster alone.

But then Eva-02 would be—

Clang!

From directly above Cinq's head came the sound of composite armor cracking and breaking.

She switched her screen to the rear-facing camera and saw something beyond all expectation—the head of a mass-production Eva with her entry plug cover clenched in its maw.

The monster's head appeared to have sprouted from her S^2 Engine's spine.

Did pushing the S^2 Engine beyond normal operation cause it to start regenerating its body?

She couldn't eject her plug now.

"So—" Cinq began to call out Asuka's name but stopped herself.

Soryu-san hasn't noticed. She's focused on her blade—too focused to detect the mass-production Eva forming behind her back.

Our best chance lies with me. There's only one thing to do. After all, I...

The mass-production Eva's newly formed arms reached out and broke Eva-0.0's neck.

Cinq cried out in pain, but no sound came.

The mental feedback link disconnected almost immediately, but the pain had been so intense that her vision blacked out.

But I haven't lost consciousness, and by all rights, I should have. Is this what they call luck? I don't actually need to see the controls to do what must be done.

"Soryu-san," Cinq said. "I gained a self, but...I'm not anybody."

I can still accelerate and move, and I can still grasp.

《What do you mean?》 Asuka didn't turn to look. She kept on cutting the hole.

"I think that I'm the part of Ayanami that she shows to the world. It's like someone took the face she wears for other people and made that into a person—or at least, that part of her is emphasized in me." Cinq paused before adding, "I'm nothing."

《I'm not sure I understand, but...》 Asuka answered as best as she knew how. 《Maybe that's how you started, but if you don't like it, you can change who you are.》

Through the vibrations, Cinq could feel Eva-02's, and Soryu-san's, determination.

《Anyway... I'll help you. We can figure it out together.》

We can?

We can!

As the mass-production Eva continued to grow, the S^2 Engine remained on the brink of self-destruction. Cinq decided to put that overwhelming power to use.

"Thank you," she said.

In the next instant, reaching out from behind Eva-02's back, Eva-0.0's laser barrel projected a tremendously powerful A.T. Field, momentarily blasting open a large hole in the Curtain.

An incredible force rocketed Eva-02 Allegorica out through the hole in the Curtain.

"That was amazing, Cinq!"

But as she flew, she turned and saw Eva-0.0 tangled up with a mass-production Eva that had grown out of its back. The monster clawed Eva-0.0 back inside the barrier and exploded in a massive cross of light.

She'd seen similar cross-shaped explosions, majestic and unsettling, many times before—whenever an Angel had been defeated.

Asuka started to call out to Cinq, but before she could, and before the radiant cross dissipated, a speeding band of light pierced its center.

It was the Lance of Longinus, 32,000 kilometers of dazzling light racing by at ninety kilometers per second.

"Not like this," Asuka said. The cross tipped over like a felled tree, bursting into tiny particles, and then it was gone. "Cinq... Not like this!"

By the time Asuka recovered from her initial shock, the lance was already tracing an arc into the distance. The hole in the barrier had closed without a trace.

"Damn it. *Damn it!*" Asuka wailed.

There was no going back. She could only go forward.

Shaken, Asuka looked to the moon, looming large.

"Have you no mercy?"

THE COMMAND CENTER witnessed Cinq's Eva-0.0 explode in a cross of light.

The ripples on the barrier were observable from Earth.

But they saw what happened next differently from how Asuka did.

The moment Asuka passed through to the other side, the Longinus Curtain changed dramatically.

The moon vanished, and the Curtain began to reflect all visible light.

In a matter of seconds, the terrestrial side of the Curtain, where the moon should have been, transformed into a mirror, the giant, concave lens reflecting the Earth, as if to say, *Humanity, gaze upon thyself.*

From that day forward, the mirror made a complete revolution once every twenty-eight days, in lockstep with the moon.

Communications and telemetry data from the lunar sortie had been cut off from the moment Cinq's S^2 Engine began mutating.

All transmissions from the command center went unanswered. Asuka's Eva-02 Allegorica remained out of contact, and Cinq's Eva-0.0 had been struck by the Lance of Longinus.

In Cinq's final moments, her mental mirror link with Trois reconnected. On the ground in Hakone, Rei Trois received everything from Cinq.

When Cinq first gained self-awareness, and she ran away from her confused self.

When Cinq first saw Trois and Six from the outside.

When a boy talked to her at school.

Trois gasped. She felt the terrible pain of her neck breaking. She lost her vision, and it was all she could do to stay on her feet.

What is this feeling of worth, as if my life has a purpose? Cinq saw a light where there should have been none.

The compressed memories flooded into Trois in less than a second, and then the link disconnected.

The moment felt much too short to convey everything that Cinq had been.

But even that short window left Trois overwhelmed and feeling like she didn't know herself anymore.

"Unit Two," she said, "is alive. She passed through the Curtain toward the moon."

Trois slumped to the floor.

CHAPTER 25

TO THE NORTH

THE MIRROR ON THE CURTAIN did more than just block the moon.

The concave surface reflected a magnified image of the Earth back upon itself, and depending on the angle, it also reflected the sun from the opposite side of the Earth, turning night into day. The curved mirror concentrated the sunlight, creating bands of droughted land. Wildfires spread everywhere.

Before anyone knew what was happening, the rest of the birds had vanished, and insect populations had exploded across the globe, causing widespread damage to the forests and breadbaskets of the world.

The Earth was falling out of rhythm.

Super Eva and Shinji caught a ride north on a Russian floating dry dock vessel that passed by eastern Japan on its way to the Port of Tomakomai in Hokkaido.

This was his punishment.

He doubted he could be of any real help on this disaster relief mission, but as the UN's military advisor had said, maintaining good P.R. was still important.

En route, in the remote briefing, Shinji had been assigned to clear the port of sunken ships and—in a few, very limited areas that were confirmed to be uninhabited—to demolish buildings that had started to tip over due to soil liquification. Super Eva couldn't work just anywhere, as even the mere vibrations from its footsteps would cause further damage.

In truth, Super Eva wasn't suited for constructive tasks. The giant was simply too large. Even the act of moving was bound to destroy something. Shinji acknowledged that his assignment was about the extent of what he could do.

The floating dry dock was supposed to sail west of Cape Erimo, but unusually tall waves had caused the ship to deviate from its intended route, and it had drifted east of the cape instead. That was the last thing Shinji remembered.

Think, Shinji, what happened next?

What did Misato say?

《Shinji-kun, Cinq might—》

Yes, I remember now. Misato told me that Ayanami—Cinq, that is—and Asuka went missing.

《Cinq might be dead.》

On the other side of my entry plug's display, Misato lowered her eyes.

Steam rose from Super Eva's armor, and I looked back into the cold wind.

I remember. I ran like hell.

Rattled by the death of someone close to him, Shinji lost the ability to distinguish which parts of himself were him and which were Super Eva. Before he knew it, he was leaping from the ship into the sea.

He picked a direction at random and ran until he reached land.

According to his navigation log, he'd cut across the Kushiro Plains and reached an open, flat area.

Shinji shuddered.

Thump. His heart pounded.

The area had been named the Kushiro Plains a long time ago, but now the land was home to cropland and pastures for dozens of kilometers in every direction, dotted by a few small farm towns. Shinji wondered if he had stepped on any buildings...or anyone.

Shinji had discovered a new downside to being merged with an Eva.

Evangelions, as a rule, were easily influenced by their pilots' mental state. That alone complicated their use as tools of war. And now, with Shinji and Super Eva, the pilot and the giant had been inextricably linked. If Shinji had an episode, he couldn't be disconnected, or restrained, or simply it out.

If he let his emotions run wild, he'd become a typhoon-level catastrophe.

But isn't that why I practiced controlling my body?

"What am I doing?"

Here and there, the farmland had been scarred by earth-quakes, and Shinji began to see that every single bit of damage had been caused by him.

Focusing his mind, Shinji increased the sensitivity of his sensors.

The houses were dark and devoid of life. Had everyone evacuated?

According to the map, there was an airport and a military base nearby.

But as far as he could see, the world was completely still.

Shinji had been told that under no circumstances was he to leave his entry plug while away on this assignment.

That was fine with him. He was afraid of seeing the devastation with his own eyes.

But as Super Eva scanned his surroundings, something caught his attention far off toward the northeastern horizon.

What he saw filled him with fear.

Thump. His heart pounded.

On the other side of the flat plains lay the open sea.

In the sea was an archipelago leading to Kamchatka Peninsula beyond the horizon.

The sky there was on fire.

It was right where the tectonic plate break had occurred.

The great rift was far from where Shinji stood—even farther than he'd traveled from Hakone to Hokkaido. It lay beyond the Earth's curve. But standing near the eastern side of Hokkaido,

Shinji could see red flames spewing from the depths of the Earth and thick, black smoke drifting east.

Shinji could only imagine how gigantic the flames were. Several jets fired in a line, like panels of a folding screen, the great rift hurling Earth's insides into the sky.

"The lance is doing all that," Shinji said with wonder and terror.

The Lance of Longinus traveled through the heavens, bringing large-scale destruction to the land.

And this was the result.

If anything could be called hell, this might have been it. But the cataclysm Shinji witnessed in this moment wasn't just restricted to this corner of the world; it was a disaster playing out across the globe.

Aftershocks shook the ground, and Shinji grew even more disconcerted.

Upon landing at Tomakomai, Shinji was supposed to have been joined by a long-endurance UAV flown directly from Nerv Japan, but according to his subdisplay, the drone was nowhere near. Shinji had made landfall far off course, and the UAV's signal was distant.

Suddenly, a voice spoke through his hydrospeaker.

《Nerv Japan Super Eva.》

Thump! Shinji's heart pounded.

The voice startled him so greatly that even Super Eva's body shuddered.

《Nerv Japan Super Eva, this is UNAF-RRC3—United Nations Armed Forces Religious Riot Control, Third Brigade.》

The transmission's IFF code checked out, and the "friend" icon lit up on Shinji's display. But something about the person's Japanese—proper, yet low and gravelly—made Shinji feel like a ghost was addressing him.

《We're glad you made it, Super Eva. But you're quite far from where we expected you to arrive.》

Shinji was about to open a communications window, but he hesitated. He switched the two-way window to voice only before establishing the connection. He didn't know what made him choose to keep the video off.

Shinji gulped in the LCL and replied, "Super Eva to UNAF-RRC3. I disembarked at the wrong location. I'm sorry, but if you could give me the route to Tomakomai, I'll—"

《No need for that, Ikari Shinji. We'll come to you.》

"Huh?" This came as a surprise.

What are they saying? This isn't where I was I assigned during the briefing.

《Repeat, UNAF-RRC3 will come to you. Send us your current coordinates.》

Shinji tried to think about what this might mean.

"Are you...suggesting we meet here and then go to Tomakomai together?"

《Look around you. After the earthquakes, *everywhere* is a disaster relief zone.》

I guess, but... A chill ran down Shinji's spine. *Something isn't right!*

He felt as if hands had suddenly grabbed his shoulders from behind.

An instinctive sense of danger shouted an alarm inside Shinji, and his heart raced.

Thump!

Thump!

As if sensing Shinji's reaction, the voice said, 《Calm yourself, Ikari Shinji. If you let yourself grow frightened, they'll come.》 Then a pause. 《No, wait. You may have already summoned one. Watch your surroundings.》

Sensing a presence, Super Eva whipped around and found—nothing.

Wait, there!

With the burning eastern sky at its back, a figure lumbered across the flatlands.

The entry plug's AI scanned the figure's outline and immediately classified it as an enemy. A match that fast could only mean one thing—the Eva had seen it before.

"An Angel Carrier!" Shinji shouted.

The Carrier appeared to have emerged from the distant rift.

But why has it come here?

Thump!

Shinji recalled what the Ayanamis had said when Super Eva's heart had first begun to beat.

That heartbeat must not be. That pulse must not be written onto the parchment of time.

Just then, the Angel Carrier broke into a sprint, and Shinji reflexively drew the prog knife from his arm rail.

Is it too late for anything to be done?

What about those terrible jets of flame filling the horizon?

Armaros said, "From the great flood, the stage will be reborn."

Was the end already nigh when the lance began its orbit? Is there nothing left for Asuka and Cinq to protect?

As if remembering to report the sighting, but actually just wanting to call home, Shinji connected to the satellite and said, "This is Shinji and Super Eva to Hakone command."

Previously, the special communications channel had displayed multiple errors; the lines had been as tangled as Shinji's thoughts. But now the connection went through.

"I've encountered an Angel Carrier in eastern Hokkaido!"

《We got through!》 Hyuga responded immediately, like he'd been waiting at the ready. 《This is Hakone command. Why are you so far from the drone? We've been trying to reach you. What's your situation?》

My situation? What is my situation?

The two giants closed in on each other. Soft earth scattered in all directions under their footsteps, and what had once been orderly and beautiful cropland was trampled.

"It's an Angel Carrier. I think Super Eva's heart summoned it!"

However sketchy the UN military officer had seemed, their explanation had stuck with Shinji, because it felt like the truth.

They're probably watching me right now. Damn it!

"The Carrier is drawn to my heartbeat!"

《Wait, how can you be sure of that?》 Hyuga asked. 《You don't have any backup or long-range weapons on you, right? Keep your distance and do not engage!》

"Too late!"

It is too late. And yet we sent Asuka and Cinq away. What if Cinq died for nothing? And what if Asuka never returns from the other side of that mirror? Assuming she's even still alive.

Shinji's thoughts sank deeper into hopelessness, and his chest constricted.

Super Eva's heart—a window to higher dimensions—began to make a low rumble distinct from its beat.

《Shinji-kun!》 Hyuga shouted.

"How... How is everything so unfair?!"

Indignant rage swelled within Shinji, and Super Eva kicked off from the ground, launching its nearly 4,000-ton body at the Carrier.

The Angel Carrier swung its staff, but Super Eva dodged the attack and delivered its knee shield to the Carrier's head.

The sound was tremendous, but the attack didn't land. The Angel Carrier manifested its A.T. Field-like shield and deflected the strike.

Sparks exploded, and then Super Eva was over the shield and landing behind the Carrier.

The UNAF-RRC3 officer came back on the comm.

《Don't go west. We've got evacuees there. If you're going to fight that thing, do it where you are. SSDF from the nearby base have already finished clearing out the civilians in your area.》

Shinji was still suspicious of this unknown caller, but he couldn't risk hurting civilians.

Before Shinji's guard was back up, the Carrier thrust its staff and tripped Super Eva. Shinji yelped as his Eva fell, gouging a large divot from the ground.

The Carrier was on top of him. It pulled back the staff and spun the weapon in a loop over its head. The axe-like tip rushed down toward Super Eva's heart.

There wasn't enough time to get up, so Super Eva rolled away from the attack—not left or right, but forward toward the Carrier, putting its head underneath the monster's frame.

The Carrier had committed to the swing and couldn't arrest its motion.

The staff struck the ground where Super Eva had been, and a spray of sediment erupted.

Shinji upended the Angel Carrier from below but kept hold of its arm.

"You're a corpse!" Shinji shouted. "You're dead! What do you want my heart for?"

Perhaps being dead is exactly *why it wants my heart.*

Shinji held out his knife at the base of the monster's shoulder—inside its shield—and let the Angel Carrier's weight do the work. The gruesome sound of tearing flesh and breaking bones echoed across the pastures, and a fountain of blood sprayed out.

Shinji had amputated the Carrier's arm, including the shoulder plate with the Q.R. Signum.

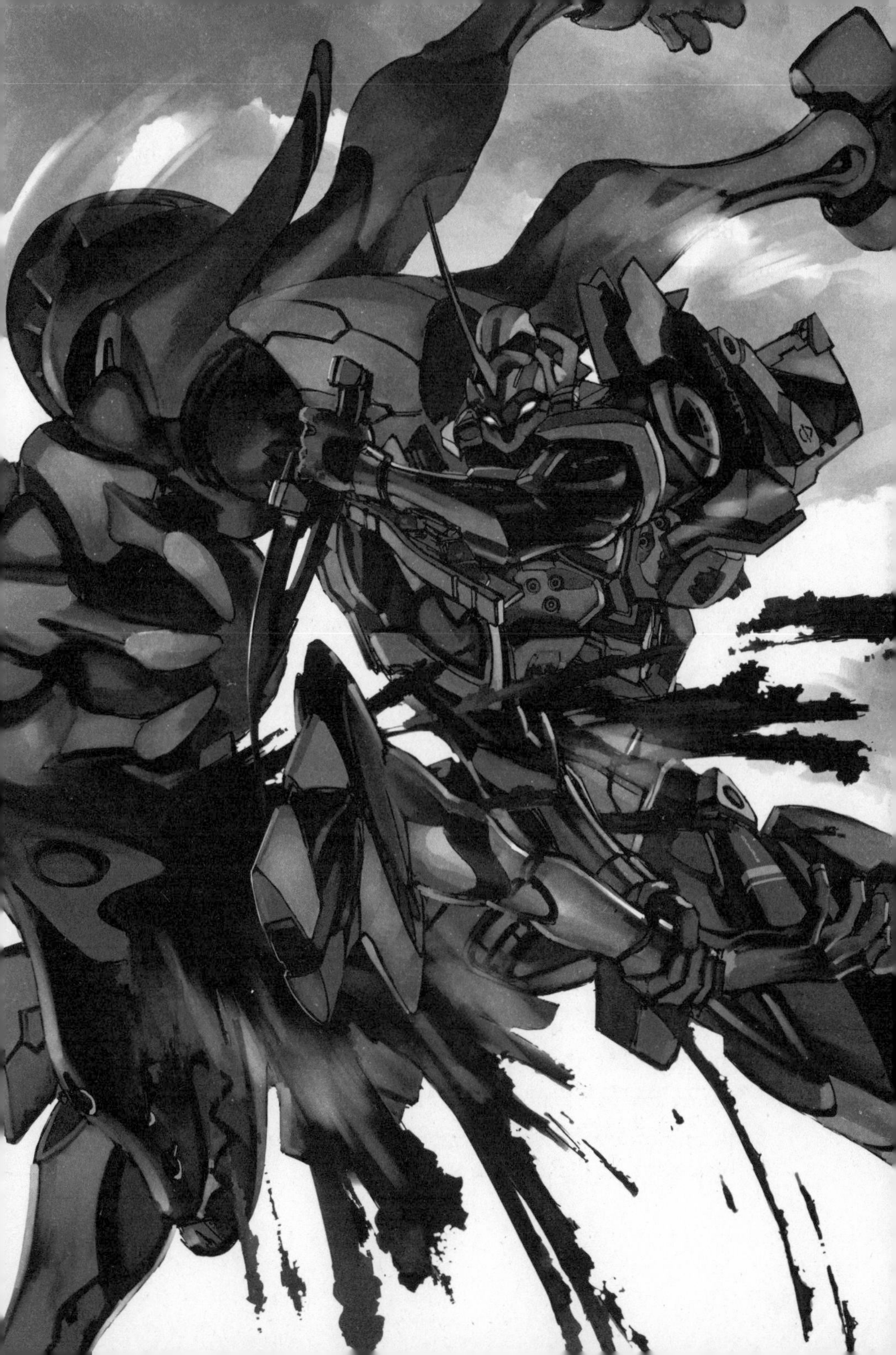

"Maybe I'd give my heart to Ayanami after her death, but I'd never give it to you!"

Would I really? Would I offer my life for her? I can't do anything if I'm dead.

Agh! Focus, Shinji!

The Angel Carrier landed on its back, and even with an arm missing, it got right back up and continued the attack.

Super Eva swung the Carrier's severed arm like a club.

The blunt force penetrated its shield surprisingly easily, crushing the giant's jaw, and it fell back on its rear.

The Q.R. Signum on the loose arm shattered into tiny crystals. Later, Shinji would realize that the Signum had allowed his grisly club to bypass the monster's shield.

Despite its many injuries, the Carrier thrust out its remaining hand, which still gripped its staff, and projected its shield at Super Eva, knocking Shinji off-balance.

Seizing the opening, the wounded white creature stood and charged, its staff pointing forward.

Shinji barely deflected the weapon's tip with his knife.

The staff slid across the edge of the blade, producing a shrill squealing, like a freight train slamming on the emergency brakes. The charging Carrier had too much momentum to be stopped, and it passed in a shower of sparks, its right shoulder hurtling toward Super Eva, the glowing Q.R. Signum projecting its shield.

Super Eva had manifested its A.T. Field in the shape of its body, and it took the blow straight on its own shoulder.

But Shinji wasn't finished.

He roared as his Eva gripped the prog knife with both hands and drove it directly into the Carrier's shoulder, putting its full weight behind the blow.

Light exploded from the surface of his opponent's shield.

The shield held, but the Carrier was no match for Shinji's rage.

Thump! Thump!

Shinji's heart pounded. His body ran hot with anger.

His knife's tip glowed with particles, making the quantum jump from the window to the higher dimensions.

As particles formed and evaporated on the blade, the knife began to pierce the Carrier's shield.

"Give Asuka back! Give Cinq back!"

Shinji forced the blade through the shield. The tip neared the Carrier's remaining Q.R. Signum and—

The black-red plate shattered, spraying crystalline fragments like blood.

The Angel Carrier returned to death. Its white corpse fell toward Super Eva, and Shinji let it roll to the side.

《Watch out!》 Misato shouted. 《You haven't dealt with the cocoon!》

No sooner had she spoken than two of the Angel Shamshel's tentacles lashed out from the Carrier's abdomen, catching Shinji by surprise and coiling around Super Eva.

Something overhead fired four shots.

Shinji barely had time to fortify his A.T. Field before a rain of tungsten-core rods pierced everything around him. Stronger than steel, dense as gold, the projectiles descended at the speed of sound.

Shinji yelped as countless rods struck his A.T. Field.

His field stopped them, but the force of their impact drove Super Eva to its knees. By the time the dust settled, Shamshel's larval body had been turned into a bloody pincushion.

The destruction had been technological—a human weapon. "The UN?"

They saved me, Shinji thought. But the attacks weren't over. The Nerv Japan drone had finally arrived, only to be shot down by an anti-air missile.

Super Eva swiveled in the direction of the missile's launch.

Shinji swept his sensors across the landscape, but everything seemed hazy.

A black cloud hung low in the northern sky.

Am I seeing things?

A section of the cloud descended in a funnel, which quickly evaporated, revealing a white-winged giant suspended in midair.

"An Eva," Shinji said softly.

From a distance, it strongly resembled the Stage 2 Eva-02, and though this giant didn't have four legs, its wings looked a lot like Allegorica's. This Eva likely carried the same type of N_2 reactor and graviton thrusters.

The Unit-02 Eva looked down on him like a guardian angel.

Reflexively, Shinji said the name of a person he thought he'd lost.

"Asuka."

A voice came from the Eva.

《Asuka still lives.》

A strange feeling came over Shinji. The voice was familiar.

《I know she lives.》

"Wait," Shinji said, finally placing it. "Hikari?"

The voice belonged to his classmate and former class representative, Horaki Hikari.

Shinji thought he heard Kaworu speak.

A flowing river would sooner reverse course than humans would stop erring. The seventeenth Angel sounded disappointed. *Even in times like this, they fight each other.*

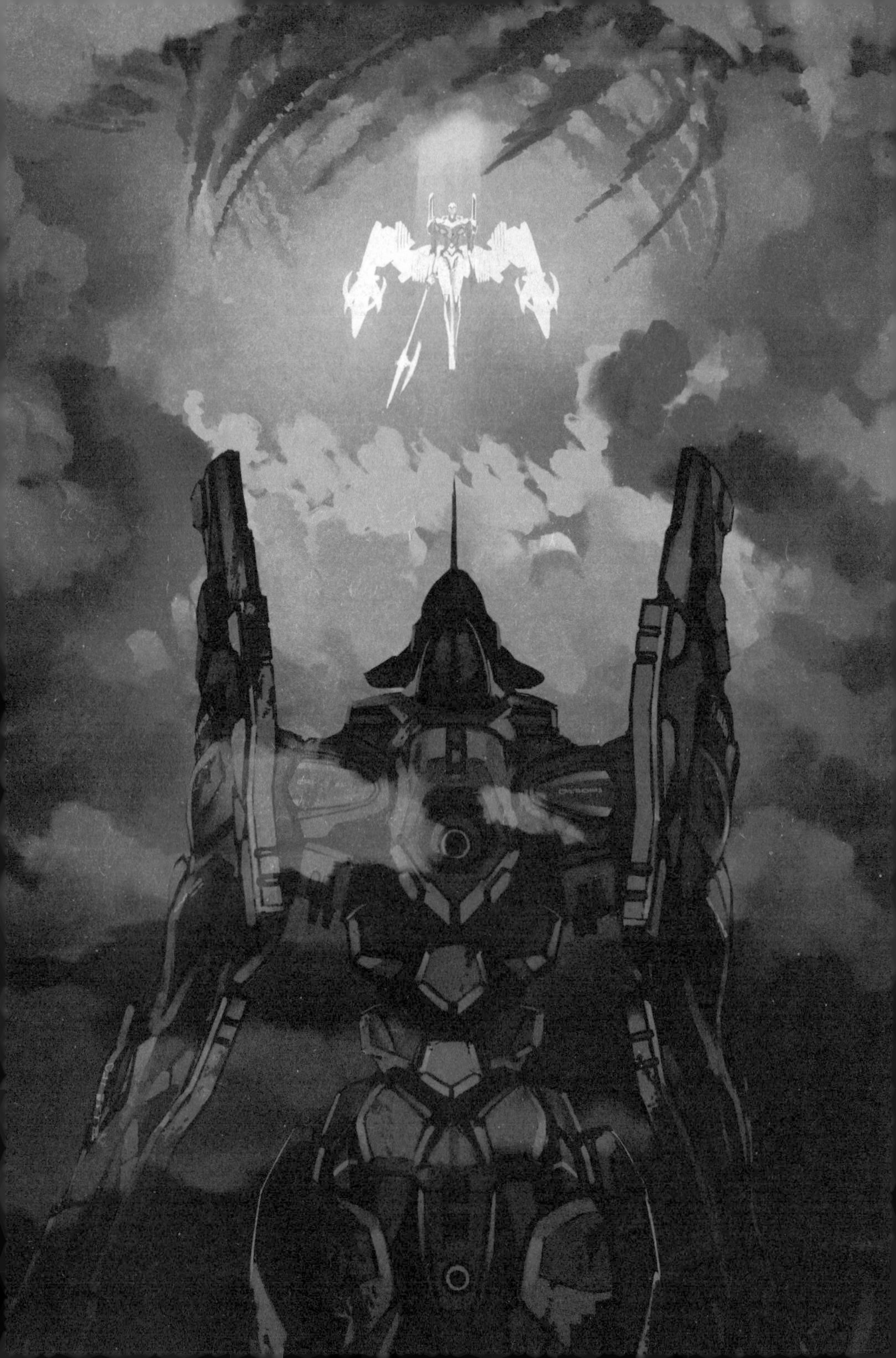

OMAKE

NEON GENESIS

CONCEPT GALLERY

EVANGELION: ANIMA

ANIMA begins with Eva-01 in the Type-F configuration from the video game (and not as it was for the anime).

A samurai with sleeves pulled up with cords and a tucked-in hakama.

There isn't a particular connection to the video game, but by including the Type-F in the story, I was able to get the publisher, *Dengeki Hobby Magazine*, to make model versions. Think of the story as beginning with Eva-01 having a somewhat atypical look.

The Unit-01 Type-F is replaced by Super Evangelion and doesn't appear in the story again, but Nerv Japan retains the Unit-00 Type-F for Ayanami Rei Trois' use—until it, too, undergoes a significant redesign and is given new pilot data.

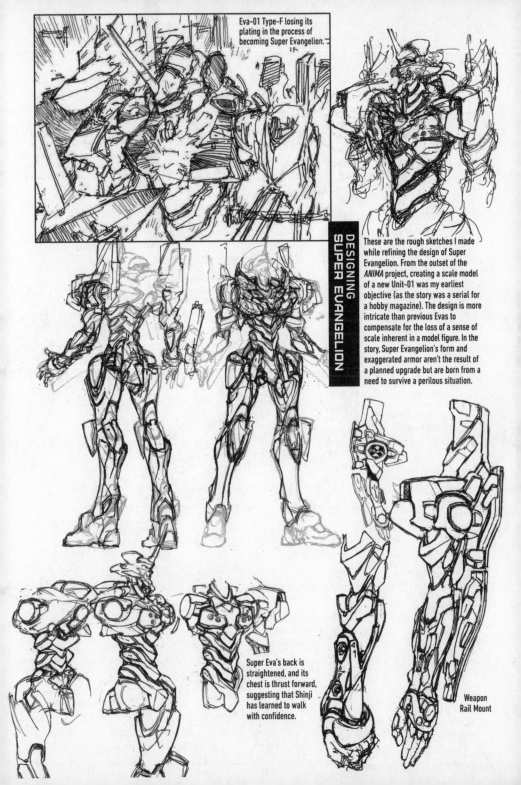

Eva-01 Type-F losing its plating in the process of becoming Super Evangelion.

These are the rough sketches I made while refining the design of Super Evangelion. From the outset of the *ANIMA* project, creating a scale model of a new Unit-01 was my earliest objective (as the story was a serial for a hobby magazine). The design is more intricate than previous Evas to compensate for the loss of a sense of scale inherent in a model figure. In the story, Super Evangelion's form and exaggerated armor aren't the result of a planned upgrade but are born from a need to survive a perilous situation.

Super Eva's back is straightened, and its chest is thrust forward, suggesting that Shinji has learned to walk with confidence.

Weapon Rail Mount

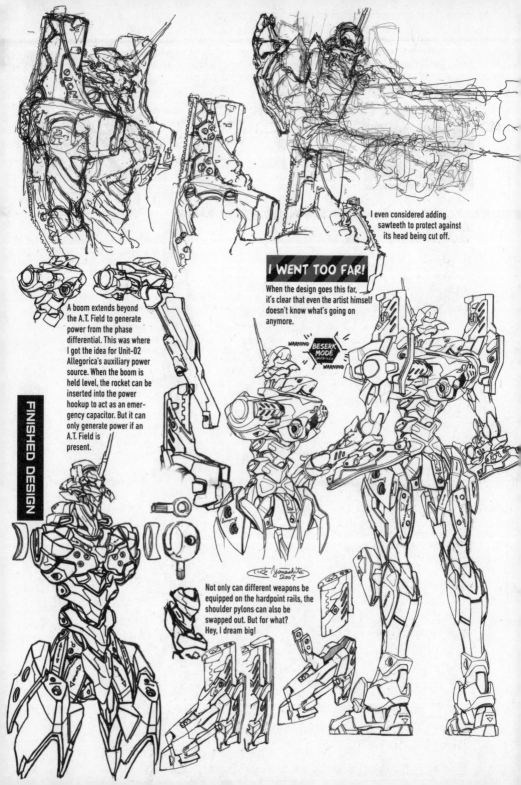

I even considered adding
sawteeth to protect against
its head being cut off.

I WENT TOO FAR!

When the design goes this far,
it's clear that even the artist himself
doesn't know what's going on
anymore.

WARNING BESERK MODE WARNING

A boom extends beyond
the A.T. Field to generate
power from the phase
differential. This was where
I got the idea for Unit-02
Allegorica's auxiliary power
source. When the boom is
held level, the rocket can be
inserted into the power
hookup to act as an emer-
gency capacitor. But it can
only generate power if an
A.T. Field is
present.

FINISHED DESIGN

Not only can different weapons be
equipped on the hardpoint rails, the
shoulder pylons can also be
swapped out. But for what?
Hey, I dream big!

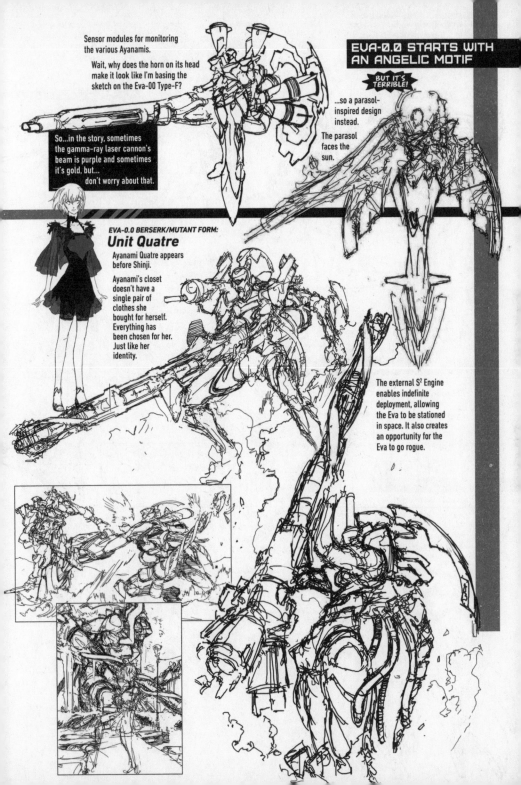

Sensor modules for monitoring the various Ayanamis.

Wait, why does the horn on its head make it look like I'm basing the sketch on the Eva-00 Type-F?

So...in the story, sometimes the gamma-ray laser cannon's beam is purple and sometimes it's gold, but... don't worry about that.

EVA-0.0 STARTS WITH AN ANGELIC MOTIF

BUT IT'S TERRIBLE!

...so a parasol-inspired design instead.

The parasol faces the sun.

EVA-0.0 BERSERK/MUTANT FORM:
Unit Quatre

Ayanami Quatre appears before Shinji.

Ayanami's closet doesn't have a single pair of clothes she bought for herself. Everything has been chosen for her. Just like her identity.

The external S² Engine enables indefinite deployment, allowing the Eva to be stationed in space. It also creates an opportunity for the Eva to go rogue.

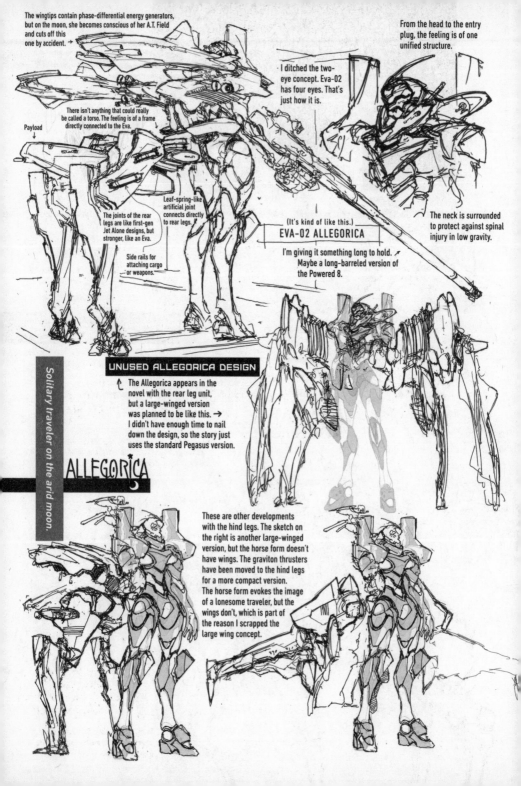

The wingtips contain phase-differential energy generators, but on the moon, she becomes conscious of her A.T. Field and cuts off this one by accident. →

From the head to the entry plug, the feeling is of one unified structure.

I ditched the two-eye concept. Eva-02 has four eyes. That's just how it is.

There isn't anything that could really be called a torso. The feeling is of a frame directly connected to the Eva.

Payload

Leaf-spring-like artificial joint connects directly to rear legs.

The joints of the rear legs are like first-gen Jet Alone designs, but stronger, like an Eva.

Side rails for attaching cargo or weapons.

(It's kind of like this.)

EVA-02 ALLEGORICA

I'm giving it something long to hold. Maybe a long-barreled version of the Powered 8.

The neck is surrounded to protect against spinal injury in low gravity.

UNUSED ALLEGORICA DESIGN

↖ The Allegorica appears in the novel with the rear leg unit, but a large-winged version was planned to be like this. → I didn't have enough time to nail down the design, so the story just uses the standard Pegasus version.

ALLEGORICA

These are other developments with the hind legs. The sketch on the right is another large-winged version, but the horse form doesn't have wings. The graviton thrusters have been moved to the hind legs for a more compact version. The horse form evokes the image of a lonesome traveler, but the wings don't, which is part of the reason I scrapped the large wing concept.

These parts are half-transparent and can only be seen when they glow.

ARMAROS

THE BLACK ARMAROS

I asked Hideaki Anno if I could use a design from the *Rebuild of Evangelion* movies for Armaros' head.

The elusive giant who orders humanity to exit the stage.

The two plates extending down to the ground from Armaros' back became a distinctive feature of its design. Before that, I had thought to give it four legs, like the Eva-02 Allegorica.

To be honest, I never finalized a single design, so every time Armaros appears, it looks different.

VARIOUS WEAPONS

Pallet Rifle / Powered 8

FOLDED RAILGUN

The figure-eight loop is intended to dampen the recoil from the bullets' acceleration. The parts of the shells that are in contact with the rail are aluminum and depleted uranium. The rail breaks after roughly two extended magazines.

Yamashita 2007

Magazine

Ground Contact Points
(When set on a level surface.)

RCRS Compatible

POWERED 8 FRAME

Because the rifle draws power from the Eva, the weapon can still be operated in this compact version (without a capacitor). Can be carried on the hardpoint rail.

◄ Barrel

MAGAZINE

├── 12 Rounds ──┤

The magazine contains stacks of 12 rounds. Because the firing rate is so fast, there is a short pause every 12 rounds as the next stack moves into place. Each magazine contains groups of rounds arranged in a 3x2x2 grid, for a total of 144 rounds. At the fastest firing speed, each set of 12 is fired almost simultaneously, and the 144 shots actually feel like 12 shots.

Empty Space

The sides of the barrel open out at an angle to dampen the shock waves and direct them upward.

◄── Barrel

Empty Space

Ground Contact Points

RCRS (Removable Connected Rail System)
All the rails are compatible with the shoulder rails.

POWERED 8 CARBINE

The barrel and accelerator are shorter, but the rifle has built-in capacitors that free the weapon from relying entirely on the Eva's power. By pulsing energy in bursts, the rifle is capable of firing more rapidly.

PROG KNIFE

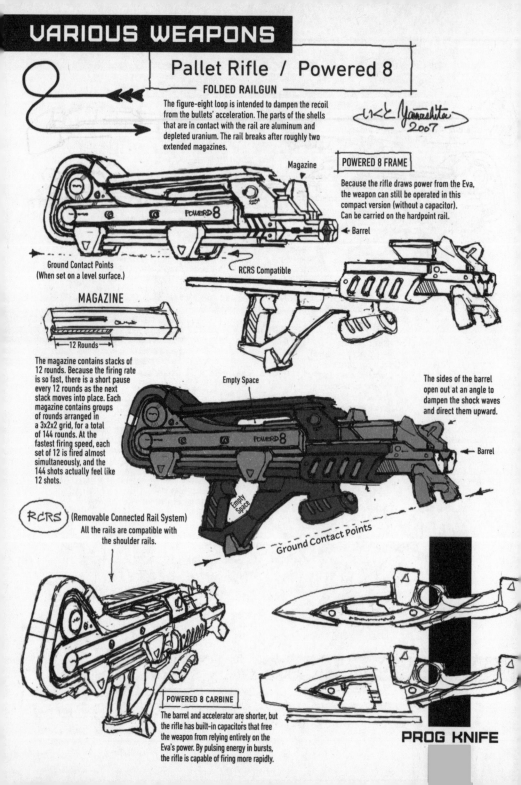

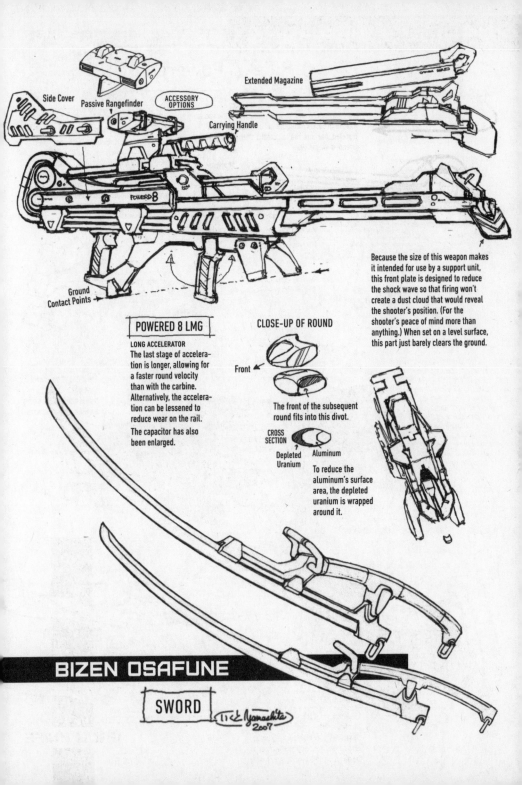

Side Cover

Passive Rangefinder

ACCESSORY OPTIONS

Extended Magazine

Carrying Handle

POWERED 8

Ground Contact Points →

Because the size of this weapon makes it intended for use by a support unit, this front plate is designed to reduce the shock wave so that firing won't create a dust cloud that would reveal the shooter's position. (For the shooter's peace of mind more than anything.) When set on a level surface, this part just barely clears the ground.

POWERED 8 LMG

LONG ACCELERATOR
The last stage of acceleration is longer, allowing for a faster round velocity than with the carbine. Alternatively, the acceleration can be lessened to reduce wear on the rail.

The capacitor has also been enlarged.

CLOSE-UP OF ROUND

Front ←

The front of the subsequent round fits into this divot.

CROSS SECTION

Depleted Uranium   Aluminum

To reduce the aluminum's surface area, the depleted uranium is wrapped around it.

BIZEN OSAFUNE

SWORD

Tick Yamashita 2007

I thought that if every Ayanami shared the same memories, they would end up identical, even as individuals. But Six's physical age created a contrast in her curiosity and ability to concentrate, which resulted in an interesting character.

heh heh heh!

heh heh!

Asuka, after the Lance of Longinus was stolen from her.

FAMILIAR [BUT NEW] CHARACTERS

Utatane-sensei handled the character designs and the title page character illustrations for the serialized version. But for this edition, the character illustrations fell to me, so they may feel a little different from what readers are used to. I hope you understand.

New Plugsuit Design

Before Shinji was given long hair.

As communication becomes increasingly difficult, Toji ends up being a major help.

My editor came up with the idea of having four Ayanamis and also their naming system. Sorry they didn't all get to be together in a lighthearted school scene.

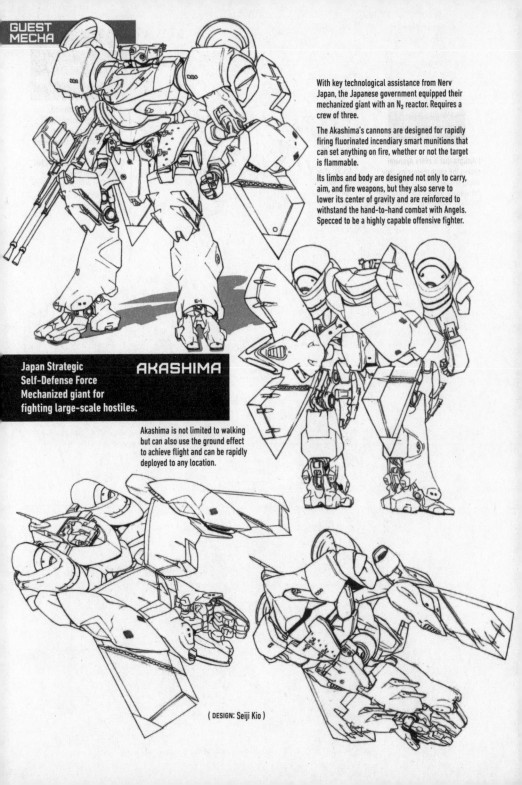

With key technological assistance from Nerv Japan, the Japanese government equipped their mechanized giant with an N_2 reactor. Requires a crew of three.

The Akashima's cannons are designed for rapidly firing fluorinated incendiary smart munitions that can set anything on fire, whether or not the target is flammable.

Its limbs and body are designed not only to carry, aim, and fire weapons, but they also serve to lower its center of gravity and are reinforced to withstand the hand-to-hand combat with Angels. Specced to be a highly capable offensive fighter.

Japan Strategic Self-Defense Force Mechanized giant for fighting large-scale hostiles.

AKASHIMA

Akashima is not limited to walking but can also use the ground effect to achieve flight and can be rapidly deployed to any location.

(DESIGN: Seiji Kio)

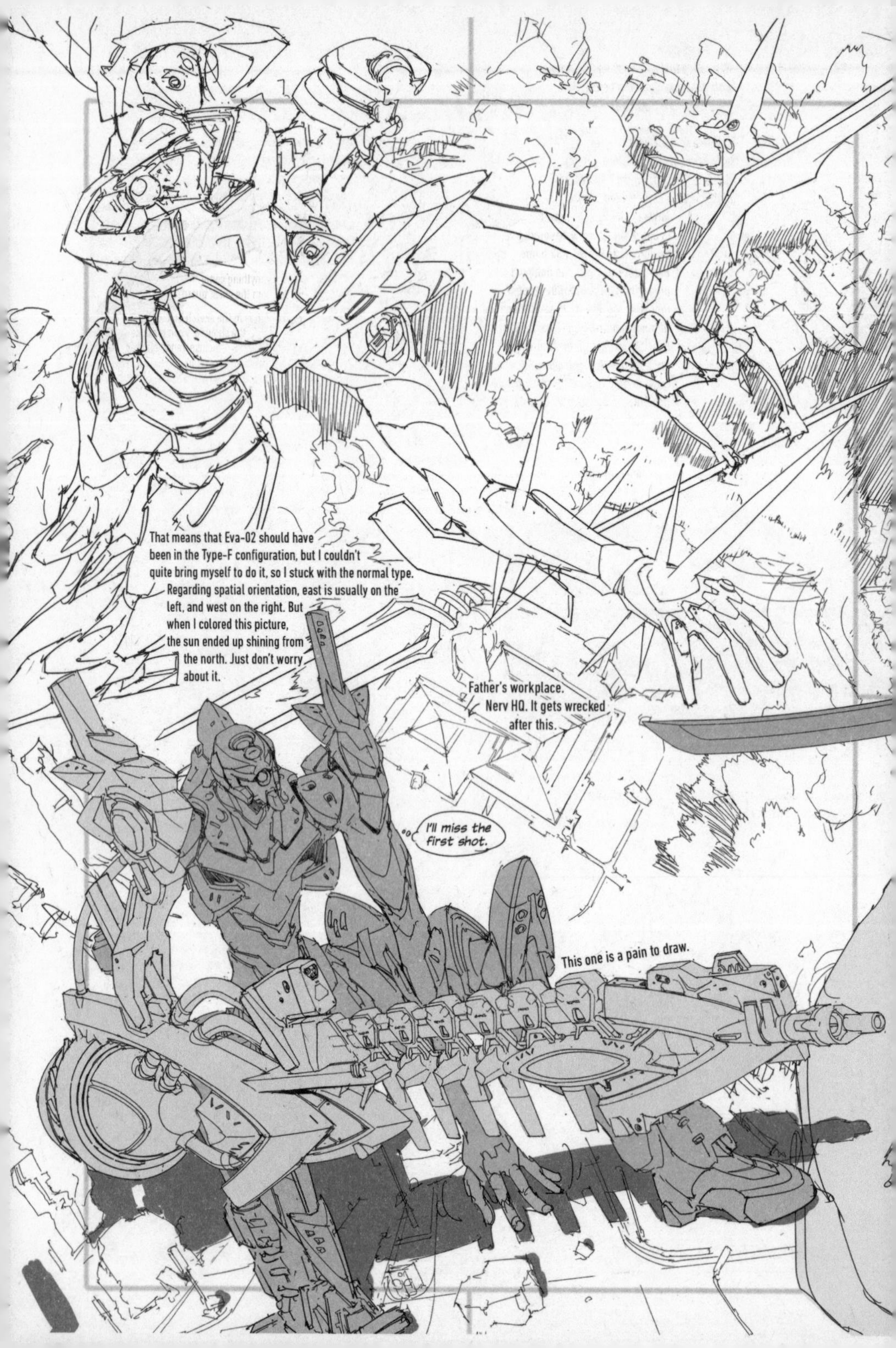
That means that Eva-02 should have been in the Type-F configuration, but I couldn't quite bring myself to do it, so I stuck with the normal type.
Regarding spatial orientation, east is usually on the left, and west on the right. But when I colored this picture, the sun ended up shining from the north. Just don't worry about it.
Father's workplace. Nerv HQ. It gets wrecked after this.
I'll miss the first shot.
This one is a pain to draw.

What are you doing starting the story with the Type-F version of Eva-01?! *This thing isn't an Eva!*

Or at least that's what I think some people will be saying... (Actually, *"This thing isn't an Eva!"* might be good copy for the cover.)

← Lake Ashi

Anyway, the Eva-01 Type-F is based on a heavy-armored design made for the PS2 game *Evangelion 2.* Later, the hobbyist magazine *Dengeki Hobby* made a model of the Eva-01 Type-F, which led to me designing Type-F variants of Eva-02 and Eva-00 that were also published in the magazine. So, when it came time to start work on *ANIMA*, my editor suggested we go with the Type-F versions.

For the cover, the publishers requested I draw the standard Eva-01. In the story, Eva-01 transforms into Super Eva very early on, but I hope it's okay that the Type-F only appears the one time...

Q Does anything come out from the chest guard?

A No. But as in the sketch below, the shoulders can produce a close-range electric attack. The technology involved (folding an A.T. Field to generate a difference in electric potential) becomes a power source for Eva-02 Allegorica.

An eel...?!

Prog knife and impact bolt (phase contrast electric weapon). *(What part of this is a knife?)*

No one remembers what the Type-F looked like, so why not add a mask?

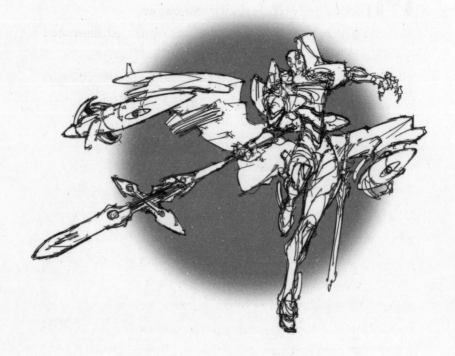

**TO BE
CONTINUED...**